PRETTY TWISTED

GINA BLAXILL lives in London. She has an English degree from Cambridge University and now works in schools liaison, helping teenagers puzzle out the mysteries of higher education. Between the ages of eleven and fifteen she wrote an epic thirty-six-part story featuring over 1,000 characters – she still remembers most of their names!

Pretty Twisted is Gina's first novel for young adults.

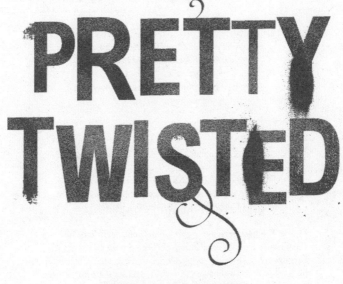

PRETTY TWISTED

GINA BLAXILL

MACMILLAN

First published 2011 by Macmillan Children's Books
a division of Macmillan Publishers Limited
20 New Wharf Road, London N1 9RR
Basingstoke and Oxford
Associated companies throughout the world
www.panmacmillan.com

ISBN 978-0-330-53327-0

1 3 5 7 9 8 6 4 2

A CIP catalogue record for this book is available from the British Library.

Printed and bound in the UK by CPI Mackays, Chatham ME5 8TD

To my wonderful parents, Sheila and David,
and to the memory of Rudi Everton Star

Jonathan
Sunday 26 October, 10.45 a.m.

We were shown into the police-station waiting room. Mum and Dad sat down, but I stayed on my feet. Apart from being worried, I was angry – at myself. Freya had been missing since Saturday 18th – a whole eight days, yet stupid me had delayed reporting it for a week, thinking I could play detective. What an idiot I'd been! This wasn't about us any more. If Freya had been abducted, a day could make all the difference, and if she ended up dead, it would be my fault.

I glanced at my parents, wondering how they were managing to stay calm. For a moment I imagined how we must appear to someone walking into the room. Dad, broad-shouldered, bearded, obviously an outdoors type, dressed in jeans, sweater and peaked cap that had all seen better days. He wouldn't have looked out of place in a farmyard. Mum, older than most mothers of teenagers, neatly but plainly dressed, thick red hair, no make-up, no jewellery aside from her wedding ring. She was wearing her best coat, but somehow it seemed shabby in the brightly lit room.

And me? A stranger would have seen a skinny sixteen-year-old wearing glasses, taller than his parents, quietly spoken – not the kind of kid who got dragged into police stations. I wasn't as good at keeping my feelings from showing as Mum and Dad were. A stranger might think I looked tense – upset – guilty even.

Normally this time on a Sunday Mum would be cooking a roast, and maybe crumble and custard if we were lucky. Family or a neighbour might drop round, and if it was cold Dad would make sure there was a log fire. Suddenly more than anything I wanted to go home, back to that safe world where I could be an ordinary teenager again. It felt surreal to be here in this white, windowless room, part of something most people just read about in the news.

'Why do the police want to speak to me again?' I asked, kicking my heels against the wall. 'I told them everything yesterday. They should be out finding Freya, not mucking about with more questions.'

'We'll find out soon enough,' Dad said. 'No point getting nervous.'

But I was nervous. And when we were shown into the interview room and Detective Inspector Shaw and Detective Sergeant Turner appeared, I could see I was right to be. Shaw's eyebrows were drawn together in a frown, and she'd pulled her hair into a tight ponytail, as though to signal she meant business. Turner, about ten years younger and a good six inches taller, wasn't smiling either. There was another man with them, whom Shaw introduced as DS Young, from Richmond CID. He looked ordinary, rather like someone's dad, but I knew his presence couldn't be a good thing.

'We're holding this interview, Jonathan, because a number of things have come to light. Before we proceed, however . . .'

Turner cleared his throat. 'You do not have to say anything. But it may harm your defence if you do not mention when questioned something which you later rely on in court. Anything you do say may be given as evidence.'

I glanced at Mum and Dad. They looked as startled as I felt.

'What's this for?' Mum asked. 'Jonathan hasn't done anything.'

'Procedure,' said Shaw. 'There are questions we're not authorized to ask without issuing a caution. If you'd like a solicitor, you're entitled to one.'

'I don't think we need that,' said Mum, eyeing Dad.

He shook his head. 'No. Jonathan has nothing to hide.'

'So, Jonathan,' said Shaw, 'we've done a thorough inspection of Freya's aunt's house. I understand Freya's been living there since September. Your fingerprints are everywhere – not surprising, perhaps – but when we entered we found that someone had put the week's post on a table by the door. Was that you?'

'Ah. Yeah, it was.'

'You should have told us you'd been in the house. The investigation team has been wasting time on a false line of inquiry because of that.'

'Sorry,' I mumbled.

'Why were you in the house?'

'I went there on Friday. You know, when I was trying to figure out if Freya was missing, before coming to you. I was only checking things out.'

'How did you get in?'

'There's a key hidden outside. Freya told me about it.'

'Did you touch anything?'

'Her phone . . . and her laptop. That was where I looked at Freya's email – you know, to see if she'd sent any messages since she vanished, like I told you.'

'You didn't mention this was done from the house.'

'Is this relevant?' asked Mum. 'And how do you know that the fingerprints are Jonathan's?'

Shaw folded her arms, face implacable.

'We have your son's DNA and fingerprints on record. This isn't the first time you've been questioned by the police, is it, Jonathan?'

I felt myself go pale.

'That was back in February.' Dad started to look angry. 'What does this have to do with Freya?'

Shaw leaned forward, arms now on the table. 'Where were you the night Freya vanished, Jonathan? I imagine you were quite upset, given she'd just dumped you.'

'Of course I was! I loved her—'

'Did you go to a friend's, perhaps?' Turner gave me a

quick smile, and I wondered if Shaw had instructed him to play good cop to her bad.

'No. Like you said, I was upset. I didn't want to go home and tell Mum and Dad what had happened so I hung around in London.'

'All night?' Shaw raised her eyebrows.

'Yeah. I missed the last train home.'

'Where did you go?'

'Down by the river near Freya's aunt's, then central London and Liverpool Street station. I got the first train home to Norfolk.'

'Can anyone confirm this?'

Mum gasped, and I jerked back in my chair.

Shaw leaned even further forward. 'Did you hang around outside Freya's aunt's house, hoping you could see her? Did you intercept Freya when she left?'

'No!'

'Are you sure?'

'Of course he's sure!' Dad snapped. 'What exactly are you implying?'

'Nothing,' said Shaw. 'All we're observing is that February's incident suggests your son has a bit of a temper – and that he's capable of taking it out on people who upset him. There's no doubt he was angry with Freya on the night in question. Several witnesses heard him shouting at her and calling her a, quote, "selfish bitch".'

'And in our experience of missing people,' Turner said, 'it's often the last person to see them who knows more than they're letting on.'

'Well, that's not what happened here, cos she's not dead and I'd never hurt her! Unless . . .' I stopped, feeling myself go cold. 'Oh God.'

Shaw and Turner exchanged a glance. Mum reached out to clutch my hand.

'You've found a body, haven't you?' I asked. 'She's dead.'

'No, nothing like that,' said Turner, and I felt my heart beat again.

Turner handed Shaw a file. From it she took two photographs and pushed them across the table.

'Do you know either of these women?'

I looked at each in turn. 'That girl's missing, isn't she?' I said, recognizing the face I'd seen a few days back in the newspaper. 'Lyndsey . . . Brown, right? The other doesn't ring any bells.'

For the first time DS Young spoke. 'Have you ever met either of them?'

'No, of course not.'

'What about Freya? Were they her friends?'

'Wait a moment,' Mum interrupted. 'Who are these girls?'

'Haven't you been watching the news, Mrs Oxley?' asked Turner. 'Both these girls were abducted from the streets of south-west London, we believe by the same person. One lived a few streets away from Freya. We found her body floating in the Thames.'

The colour drained from Mum's face. 'Oh God. You think there's a connection with Freya.'

'Impossible to say, but we're treating this as suspicious.' Shaw turned back to me and I shook my head.

'Far as I know, Freya never met these girls.'

'Where were you on the night of Saturday the twenty-seventh of September, Jonathan? Four weekends back.'

'I was . . . well, I was visiting Freya. We went to a concert and got back to her aunt's late-ish.'

'Can the aunt confirm this?'

'Think she was asleep.'

'So Freya's the only one who can corroborate your story.'

'We spoke to people at the concert – but after then, yeah. What does this have to do with anything?'

The police looked at me coolly, and in a flash I realized. The newspaper report I'd read about that girl said the last time she'd been seen was on Saturday 27 September. I remembered the date because it was Freya's birthday weekend. The police couldn't think . . . surely not?

I turned to Mum and Dad. I was starting to feel dizzy and knew I had to get out before I said something stupid. 'Can we please go home now?'

'We haven't finished yet,' said Shaw, and she sounded

so serious that I began to sweat. My actions did look suspicious – for all the police knew, I could have been deleting evidence when I looked at Freya's phone and laptop – and they clearly hadn't ruled out the idea that I'd waited outside her house and done something terrible to her . . .

Scariest of all, I realized there was no evidence to prove I hadn't. No one had seen me that night and, heck, Freya's mates had even heard us arguing! The boyfriend was always the number-one suspect when a girl vanished. How many times had I seen distraught guys making appeals on the news, only to be charged with murder a few days later? God, I wished I hadn't named Lyndsey – that looked super-dodgy, especially as I had no alibi for the night she vanished either. What a nightmare this was turning into.

Rosalind
11.45 a.m.

It seemed like I'd been waiting ages. I mooched from my bedroom to the kitchen to the sitting room, then back again. Olivia came out of her room, trying to text and button up her jacket at the same time. She asked me what I was doing. I couldn't answer – because I really didn't know any more. I shouldn't even have been part of this.

The reception had been bad when Jonathan had called me earlier. I had difficulty making out what he was saying.

'Police?' I asked. 'But they've already spoken to you about Freya.'

'Maybe they're suspicious about the time we wasted before reporting her missing,' Jonathan said. 'Don't worry, Ros, I haven't told them about you – no reason for you to get involved.'

I wished I had something comforting to say when he called back, but I was more tangled up in this than he realized. He hadn't guessed yet – despite all the lies I'd told him, he trusted me. I almost wished he didn't. I could toughen up and tell myself it didn't matter if he thought I was a crazy, sick person – because that's what he would think if he knew that I'd followed – stalked – Freya round London that day. He'd want to know why I did it, and telling him that would be the worst thing imaginable.

Funny to think that a couple of months ago I'd been wishing everything would change. Now I was almost wishing I'd never let Jonathan into my life.

I lay on my bed and stared at the stain on my ceiling from when a tile fell off the roof and the rain came in. If you looked at it in a certain way, it was shaped like Great Britain. Dad had been promising to do something about it for months, but of course he hadn't.

My phone rang. It was Jonathan.

'Ros?'

He sounded dazed, and I wished I was there so I could hug him. I pulled myself off the bed and closed the door. Olivia had gone by now so there was no one home to overhear, but I felt safer with it shut.

'Jono! Are you OK? What did they say?'

He drew breath, and I knew what he was thinking even before he said it.

'Ros, how the hell did we get into this mess?'

1. Online

Rosalind
Saturday 30 August, 10.00 p.m.

In the moments you need contact with a human being, there's never the right person there.

Strangely, when I had this thought, I was hardly alone. It was ten o'clock on Saturday night and I was hanging out round the back of the bowling alley with my best friend, Abby, Claudia Rowley-Wood and a bunch of Claudia's hangers-on I didn't know. Abby was crouched in a corner, giggling. Whether she was drunk on the few mouthfuls she'd taken from the bottle of Smirnoff Ice we'd passed round or just pretending, I couldn't tell. Claudia, unnecessarily dolled up for an evening in a grubby alleyway, was baiting two of the boys with a packet of fries.

'Time for art class.' One of the guys opened a plastic bag to reveal multicoloured spray cans.

'We could go to the park,' another said. 'The wall at the back of the tennis courts has just been repainted. It's begging for some decoration.'

'What should I write, Claudia?' Abby, equipped with green spray, managed to make the question sound like begging. Claudia tilted her head and pursed her well-glossed lips. It sickened me to see Abby, a self-styled goth who talked about 'standing out', acting like a faithful dog, so I joined the graffiti boys. They were laughing and spraying the wall, thinking they were being clever. Even though I was aware that someone would have to clean this off, I pressed the nozzle. I knew what would happen, but was still surprised when a splodge of bright orange appeared on the wall. The splodge turned into a curve, and I joined the curves to make a figure. It was easily recognizable as a woman wearing a ball gown. Her face I left blank.

I would have drawn her a partner if the others hadn't got restless. We trailed out, across the car park and on to the pavement leading away from the retail park. For a Saturday night it was quiet, with only a few cars and a bus on the normally busy road. The noise we were making seemed to carry a long way. I walked alongside Abby, but she was too busy sharing Claudia's cigarette and trying hard not to look like it was the first time she'd smoked to pay me any attention. A middle-aged couple saw us coming and crossed over the road.

'Are we hanging out tomorrow?' said Abby.

Claudia made a pretence of considering this. I ground my teeth together. *Of course* we were hanging out tomorrow. Claudia's crew spent every Sunday on the benches outside Tesco.

'S'pose so,' said Claudia, making it sound like a gracious handout.

'Great. Outside Tesco then. Can Ros come?'

Claudia's gaze flickered my way, then she turned, talking loudly to one of the guys as if I wasn't there.

I don't care, I thought, glaring at her back view. And I wouldn't go tomorrow, just to show I didn't care. If Abby wanted to go and act stupid, that was her problem.

We stopped outside the Malt and Hops, looking through the old-fashioned arched windows to see who was working behind the bar and whether they'd be likely to serve us. Everyone looked to Claudia for a lead – and I decided that was it. There was no way I, a fourteen-year-old who didn't even look her age, would be let in. I wasn't going to give Claudia the satisfaction of seeing me turned away.

I was expecting someone to call out and ask where I was going, but I turned off the high street without anyone noticing. I wondered how long it would take them to realize I wasn't there – if they realized at all.

I hoped Abby would phone the next morning, but she didn't. I was alone in the house, so I made pancakes with whipped cream, chocolate spread and Gummi bears on top to cheer myself up. I feel rather like Cinderella these days, stuck indoors while others are out having fun. I'm always finding notes on the table – *Remember to take the recycling bins out* or *Could you give the kitchen a clean? Thanks!* The last time we did something as a family was a long time ago. My older sister, Olivia, is always round at her boyfriend's house, and Dad has started seeing Petra, who just happens to be covering my drama teacher's maternity leave. They met at parents' evening, and I could tell at once there was something there, because Petra didn't mention that I'm heading for a D in drama unless I start being more 'sociable' and learn to work better with other students. Dad has never been an interfering parent, but thanks to Petra I barely see him now. He's started squeezing into trendy shirts and jeans and he's even planning to go to *Ibiza* with her. I mean – please! Petra's OK – friendly without being in your face, and she tells quite funny stories about people she knows in theatre – but she's still my teacher. I feel really awkward whenever we pass in the school corridor, even though Petra keeps it neutral. Thank goodness she's only at my school until half-term.

As for Mum – well, Mum's not around.

Normally I have no problem amusing myself. I like to draw people – either from memory or photographs in fashion magazines. I have sketchbooks filled with portraits. Today, though, I couldn't make the pencil do what I wanted, and I gave up. So I messed about baking a chocolate cake that sank in the middle, made myself a sandwich, then watched a romantic comedy which annoyed me so much that I turned the TV off. I'll never understand how people can enjoy films where heroines stop wearing glasses, straighten their frizzy hair and suddenly become so beautiful that everyone falls at their feet. Maybe they're living in a different world to me. The world I know is one where people let you down and happy endings don't happen.

After eating some of my cake, which tasted better than I thought it would, I went online and checked MyPlace, my favourite social-networking site. Just at that moment a message popped up, telling me that an unknown person calling themselves 'Squeebunny' was messaging me.

I hadn't used MyPlace's instant-messaging function much; I was more interested in uploading my artwork than chatting to people. Besides, I didn't know this person. 'Squeebunny': one stupid name out of billions of faceless Internet users. I moved the mouse to delete him or her. But then the message box popped up, and Squeebunny spoke.

Jonathan
10.30 p.m.

I stood at the side of the room, trying to look like I was having a good time. Sixteen-year-olds are meant to enjoy parties, and this one seemed like a good idea – it was being hosted by Tammy Whiting, whose parents were loaded. As well as most of our year, she'd invited a bunch of kids I didn't know; I guessed they must have enrolled in some of the same colleges as us. Not for the first time, I wished my school did A levels and I didn't live in the sticks. The nearest sixth-form colleges were in Norwich, a good twenty miles away. Even worse, I'd have to catch the 7 a.m. zombie bus, which everyone says is only ever on time when you're late. I couldn't wait until I could start driving lessons next summer.

I'd thought that everyone would be nervous about starting college, but I couldn't imagine that the trendily dressed, confident-looking people around me had been fretting all summer like I had. They looked alarmingly at ease, laughing in groups, already the greatest of friends. I can never think of what to say to new people – besides, they were talking about celebrities I'd barely heard of. They probably wouldn't be interested in me anyway – heck, even people I knew weren't. Two girls from my year I'd just approached had given me blank looks and said, 'Sorry – what was your name?'

'You don't know after five years in the same school?' I tried to make it a joke, but it came out sounding wrong so I added quickly, 'Jonathan. You know – Freya's boyfriend?'

Freya's name sparked some interest and we managed to talk for a while, shouting over the music – some annoying playlist of hits from talentless boy bands. I wished Freya was here; people always looked at me differently when we were together. But she had left for her aunt's house in London a few days ago and so far was having a good time. Classes at her music school hadn't begun yet, but she'd already made a number of friends. I wasn't surprised – Freya's pretty and, unlike me, always seems to know the right thing to say. She's just one of those people others warm to.

This was the first time I'd been out without her in months, I realized. It was difficult to remember how things had been before; I'd changed a lot since we'd started dating. I was surprised none of the people Freya had introduced me to were here tonight – I knew they'd been round Tammy Whiting's house before. Though they were more her friends than mine, I'd been banking on their company. I was beginning to wish I'd made an effort to keep up with my old mates; while I'd been a bit of a loner, there were a few kids I was friendly with, mainly from karate class. But they'd become distant, and if I was honest, I knew it was my fault for getting too wound up in Freya's world.

A fist connected with my stomach, making me choke on a mouthful of Archers.

'Jono! Where've you been hiding all summer?'

It was Stuart, a guy who'd been in my class. We often played battleships during RE classes and he sometimes copied my homework when rugby practice got in the way of doing it himself. While we weren't exactly mates, I was ridiculously relieved to see him.

'Wasn't hiding,' I said. 'Just didn't hang out much. Freya and I were composing stuff.'

'You look like your cat's just died. Here.' He shoved a plastic cup at me. 'Drown your sorrows.'

'What is it?'

'Cider. Go on.'

I took the cup, putting down my half-finished Archers. I don't really like cider, and I was already starting to feel pretty peculiar after the drinks I'd had earlier, but I didn't want to look a wimp in front of Stuart.

'Your girlfriend's gone to some fancy music school, right?' Stuart asked, watching me as I took a gulp of the drink. 'The Conservatory or something. Sounds well up itself.'

'It's a conservatoire, actually. The London Conservatoire.'

'Whatever. How come you're not going?'

I shrugged. 'Even aspiring rock stars need A levels. According to my parents.'

'Hey, have you heard? Tom Copeland's moved to Bury.'

I swallowed too quickly and choked.

Stuart slapped me on the back. 'My mum reckons it's your fault,' he said. 'Mrs Copeland told her she didn't want Tom having anything to do with us after what you did. Says you're dangerous.'

'Look, I don't want to talk about that. College is meant to be a new start, OK?'

It was at this point I realized a girl was standing next to me. 'Hi, Jonathan,' she said, giving me a wave.

'Uh . . . do I know you?' I asked.

'Nope, but you will, because someone told me you're taking maths at the same college I'm going to. I'm Natasha.'

'Ah, right.' There was a pause, during which I tried to think of something witty to say. I felt Stuart's elbow come into contact with my ribs.

'Lucky,' he muttered. 'She's fit.'

'I noticed,' I said, and gave Natasha a wobbly smile as I finished the cider. 'So, are you a maths whizz?'

'Far from it. Maybe you can help me out.'

'I guess I could try.'

She laughed. 'Don't be so modest! You're really smart. I've heard stories.'

I couldn't help but feel flattered. Maybe this wasn't such a bad party after all.

'What stories?' I asked.

'Freya Rose told me you used to do her maths homework for her.'

'You know Freya?'

'Yeah, we had the same violin teacher. You went out, right? I heard she'd picked up a geeky boyfriend.'

I hadn't been called a geek in a long time. Seemed a lifetime ago I'd been the guy who hid in the computer lab at lunchtime, who wore bad glasses and came top of the class. 'I still am her boyfriend.'

'Right.' Natasha looked amused. 'Somehow I can't see Freya holding up a long-distance relationship. She's had quite a lot of boyfriends, hasn't she?'

Suddenly I didn't feel quite so at ease. I shook my head when Stuart offered me another drink, beginning to wish I could get out of the room, away from all these people. 'What?'

'Nothing. Just . . . a few interesting stories about Freya came my way.'

'Well, I don't want to hear them.'

'Very loyal of you.'

Now I had no idea what she was getting at. I was trying to think of how I could reply when my head started to spin. I reached out and held on to the back of a chair.

'What's up?' I heard Natasha ask.

The faces and forms around me were fuzzy now, and I knew I had to get outside. My stomach was churning and my legs were threatening to buckle. I fought my way to the door, muttering apologies. Outside, in the cold air, I took several deep breaths, then found myself on my knees. I realized people were standing round me. Someone – Natasha – was kneeling too, her hand on my arm.

'Jonathan, are you all right?'

I wanted to say, 'I'm fine,' but instead my stomach spoke, pushing up beer, cider, Archers and everything I'd eaten, right in front of Natasha.

★

Everyone's worst nightmare and it had to happen to me.

I don't remember how I got home, but when I woke I was in bed. Not unsurprisingly, I had a pounding headache. When I picked up my mobile there was a message from Stuart.

BTW I laced ur cider with vodka, thought u needed it. Oh & u owe me 4 the taxi home. ☺

It was almost lunchtime before I felt well enough to get up. I went into the kitchen and found my parents and the Morrisons from next door sitting round the table. I wished someone had warned me we had guests before I came down in my pyjamas.

'Good night, was it?' Dad called as I went to the fridge. I could tell from the expression on his face that he was trying not to laugh. In fact, they were all looking amused.

'Fine,' I muttered, taking a carton of juice.

'Anything interesting happen?' asked Mum. I grunted. 'Would you like me to make you something to eat?'

I was hungry, but there was no way I was sticking around to be asked embarrassing questions. I grabbed a bread roll and was nearly out of the door when Dad said, 'Jonathan?'

'What?'

'It's not a good idea to mix your drinks.'

I slunk off to my room and spent the rest of the afternoon feeling stupid. College was going to be fun and games tomorrow if word spread about what I'd done. Being forgotten suddenly seemed an attractive prospect.

Mum tried to get me to come down to dinner but I didn't fancy it, especially as the Morrisons were still there. But after a while the Sunday-evening quietness started to get to me. I wanted someone to talk to. I considered phoning Freya, but there was no way I was going to tell her I'd humiliated myself.

So on a whim I turned to my laptop, logged on to MyPlace and clicked on 'Search for friends'. In the past I'd used the search tool to find and chat to people who liked the same bands as me; today I wasn't bothered who I hooked up with. I didn't bother filling in most of the details, except to limit the search to people in the UK who were online right now. I just wanted to tell someone how I was feeling, someone who I didn't know and couldn't think any less of me. Whether they replied or not didn't matter.

The first name the search tossed up was someone called 'Rozzledozzle'. I started typing.

I am a total loser. I wanted to make a good start at sixth form. Instead I got pissed and threw up over this girl.

I banged the enter key, expecting nothing to happen. I stared at my screen for a moment. Two words appeared.

so wot?

Rosalind
Sunday 31 August, 8.25 p.m.

The mild curiosity I'd felt when Squeebunny popped up on my screen disappeared the moment I saw his message. Brilliant, someone wanting to unload his crap on to me. I knew Squeebunny was a he because I'd looked at his profile: male, sixteen, Norfolk, United Kingdom. There was an arty photo of some guy playing a guitar, face turned away, and he'd written that his interests were rock music, computers and horror films, along with a lengthy list of what I guessed were bands he liked; in other words, we had nothing in common.

College is meant to be a new start and I've screwed it up, came a second message.

I almost ignored him, but boredom got the better of me. *no u havent*, I told him. *& actually ur life isnt half as screwed up as mine*.

Oh?

I didn't reply immediately. The question mark behind the 'oh' made it seem a much bigger word.

my best friend is bein rubbish. shes suddenly bcome matey wiv this gang & wants me 2 hang out wiv them. yesterday we graffitied a wall – thats the kinda thing they think is fun.

You didn't have to join in.

i no that tnx.

Did you want to fit in?

I frowned at the words, suddenly wondering if this conversation was going places I didn't want it to. *hey i no my own mind,* I typed.

Wanting to fit in doesn't mean you don't.

i didnt do wot they did. they were writin stupid stuff, i was drawin a picture.

So you were fitting in up to a point, but also letting them know you're an individual?

wot r u, some kinda shrink? i don't even like these ppl.

Sounds like you still care though.

wot exactly is ur point?

Been there myself, that's all. I've hung out with people I didn't have anything in common with for the sake of company. I was kinda doing that last night – so maybe I know how you feel.

o yeah?

Yeah. I tell myself I don't give a damn what they think, but I obviously do or I wouldn't bother with them. I can only take so much being ignored. Sometimes I think wanting to be liked is what everyone wants most.

I read the response a couple of times before replying. Maybe Squeebunny wasn't the irritating attention seeker I'd thought – I could see where he was coming from here.

im used 2 bein ignored. I decided it couldn't hurt to be

honest. It wasn't as though I was ever going to meet this guy. *it shouldnt hurt me any more. ppl have been makin assumptions bout me 4 years. i dont go round moanin, there4 they think ive nothin 2 complain about – no1 seems 2 realize i have the same feelings as they do.* ☹

I know what you mean. Because I wear glasses and get good grades and play computer games, people think I'm a swot and a geek.

yeah. i get labelled as 'miss sensible' and ppl always look 2 me when things need sorting out. i wish i wasn't like that cos sometimes its not much fun. I paused. *i guess ur right. id kinda like ppl 2 c me as i am*.

Sometimes it only takes one person thinking you're special to change the way you see things.

im no1s special person.

Sometimes I feel like that, but can I say something else?

Heck, this guy was really getting into the swing of agony uncle. I wondered if Squeebunny really was a sixteen-year-old guy – he definitely wasn't like the ones I knew at school. Who was this person – and why was he talking to me? A little warily I typed, *ok*.

I would just tell your friend she's taking you for granted. She might not have realized. Nothing beats being honest.

Huh. I thought about typing, *bein honest is hard*, but

instead, deciding I'd had enough of this weird guy, logged off.

Only then did I realize how weird it was that Squeebunny, who had messaged me to unload his problems, had ended up listening to mine.

Jonathan
9.10 p.m.

I kind of enjoyed speaking to Rozzledozzle, even if she hadn't given me much of a chance to angst at her. No one had ever listened to my advice before – people at school didn't pay me much attention, and Freya had everything sorted already.

And I decided to stop worrying. Mum had asked again and again why I always thought the worst rather than the best about things, why I beat myself up over every tiny mistake. When I saw Natasha at college I'd apologize and hope the story hadn't spread – fat chance with Stuart's big mouth – but that was all I could do.

I kind of wished Rozzledozzle hadn't logged off. I clicked on her profile. It was colourful, with fancy fonts and graphics – she'd evidently spent time customizing it. There was even a folder containing portraits, mostly of people I half-recognized from films. One of these sketches – a glam-looking girl with long curly hair with a flower in it – had been uploaded as her profile picture. Her age wasn't filled out – just a birthday, 11 July – and she hadn't listed her hobbies or favourite bands and TV shows either. Maybe she just used the page to show off her art. Despite myself, I was interested – especially as she'd written that she was from London. I wondered if she lived anywhere near Freya.

2. Busy

Jonathan
Saturday 6 September, 12.15 p.m.

I got through the first week of college – more or less. I was determined to be cheerful when I phoned Freya on Saturday.

'It's got its cons, but it's better than school,' I said. 'Missing you loads though.'

'Likewise,' said Freya. 'Bumped into anyone interesting?'

'Don't really know yet. It's weird meeting people by myself. I seemed to have so much more to say when you were around.'

'No one really makes friends in the first week. Everyone's too busy projecting an "I am normal" image to be themselves. Speaking of which, I hope you're wearing the clothes I bought you.'

I laughed. 'You mean the clothes *I* bought me when you appointed yourself my personal shopper? Yeah. My savings account is still complaining.'

'Stuff that; you needed a new wardrobe. And it's not my fault I'm programmed to spend other people's money; I'm a Libra.'

I rolled my eyes. 'So how are things going at your end?'

'Great! You'd love it here, Jonny, not having to bother about stupid things like science or geography. The teachers at the conservatoire are really laid-back – a lot of the classes are one on one, and it makes you feel as though you matter. The guy who takes me for violin is called Mark and he's just amazing – he plays with the London Symphony Orchestra.'

I glanced across at my guitar. I hadn't felt like playing recently – I'd been very off form during my lesson this week. 'Awesome.'

'The other students are fun – we went to this cafe after the first day with our violins and guitars, and there was such a buzz. And last night we went to a fancy-dress party. You know what they got me wearing? A bunny-girl outfit. I'm lucky I didn't get arrested for indecent exposure.'

'What did your aunt say?'

'Nothing. Auntie Phil's not home most of the time. Apparently my parents told her I could be trusted and that's good enough for her.'

'Wow. Catch my aunts being that accepting.' But then that was Freya all over – a complete pro at getting what she wanted. The last year at school I don't think she did a single games lesson because she had the teacher eating out of her hand.

'Shall I send you a photo of me in the bunny outfit? It might cheer you up.'

I gave another laugh – a rather half-hearted one. 'Not

sure I like the idea of other blokes seeing you like that.'

'Of course you don't, you're a Taurus. You're prone to possessiveness, did you know?'

'Not being possessive. Just wouldn't want other guys to get their hopes up, seeing as you already have a boyfriend.'

I was hoping Freya might give me some reassurance, but instead she said, 'Oh, I don't know, having some strong guys at my disposal might be useful. They can be my escorts. A girl a few streets away disappeared back in July.'

'Seriously?'

'Yeah, there are loads of posters asking for information. The police have been looking round and everything. It's a little scary.'

'I'll have to come and visit soon so I can walk you places.'

'And if anyone tries to abduct me, you can use your mad karate skillz on them.'

I sighed impatiently. 'I don't do karate any more, Freya. You know why.'

'I wish you'd stop tearing yourself up over that. The idiot deserved all you gave him.'

That was all very well for Freya, I thought. She hadn't been the one pulled in front of the police.

'Tell me more about the conservatoire,' I said. 'Do you do much composing – and did you tell people about us?'

'Of course! Mark had me sing and play one of our pieces with another student doing your guitar bit.

Everyone was very impressed.'

I wasn't sure how I felt about that. Though we'd written the music for others, the notes belonged to me and Freya.

'Sounds like another life,' I said eventually.

'Sure is. The travelling's expensive though. I've had to get a job waitressing again on Friday nights. Listen, Jonny, I've got to go now. Chat soon, OK?' Before I had a chance to ask when, she'd rung off.

Funny, I'd expected speaking to the person who meant the most to me to make me feel better, but for some reason it had done quite the opposite.

I'd had one piece of luck at college – Natasha wasn't in my maths class after all. Though there'd been a couple of jibes about the throwing-up episode, everyone was too busy to gossip about me.

As for lessons, they didn't seem difficult, though there was more homework than I'd expected. I felt a bit odd when I saw my timetable. This piece of paper would be my life for the next year. A constant cycle of maths, further maths, physics and chemistry. It felt like I'd handed over my soul to the devil.

The biggest problem, as it turned out, was the zombie bus. My parents had to drag me out of bed the first morning. I must have looked wrecked, because when they dropped me at the bus shelter Lucy Booker bobbed up and squeaked,

'Don't worry, Jonathan, I'll make sure you get to college OK.' This was a laugh considering Lucy is about a foot shorter than me and can't even look after herself properly, but I was too zoned out to argue.

Lucy insisted on plonking herself next to me on the bus and jabbered the whole journey about some website she'd discovered. I knew I should be grateful someone was being friendly, but I was a bit embarrassed that it was Lucy. Not very long ago she'd been my female equivalent. She got on well with the teachers, played 'geeky' video games and even wore glasses like mine. Our class made endless jokes about how perfect we were for each other.

That evening I decided to have an exciting night in watching naff eighties music videos on the Internet. I'd just made a cup of tea when a message popped up at the bottom of my screen: Rozzledozzle had come online.

Hey, I typed, opening a conversation. Remember me?

yeah.

Wondered if you felt like chatting.

Rozzledozzle didn't reply. I wasn't entirely surprised. But then, after about fifteen minutes, a new message popped up.

i did wot u said.

Oh yeah?

yeah. the more i thought bout it the more it made sense so i told abby she was bein a crap friend.

What happened?

she wouldnt take it. she even tried 2 get me 2 feel sorry 4 claudia by tellin me her parents were separating. so wot? my parents divorced but i never used it as an excuse 2 b a bitch!

I wasn't sure how to respond to this. Luckily another message popped up.

i dont think abby understands how i feel at all. ☹ she always takes me 4 granted, & im sposed 2 b her best friend.

That sucks. So you didn't manage to resolve anything?

we r givin each other space atm. itd b OK if i had other friends 2 hang round wiv but i dont. its always just been us ever since primary skool. its funny, i thought standin up 4 myself wd feel better than this.

Suddenly I felt odd. My words had changed the life of someone I didn't know. Mind me asking your age?

A pause. *16*.

Same here. I think a lot of things go weird around our age. Everyone's moving in different ways.

i dont mind things changin. i just want them 2 change 4 the beta.

The new people thing might be one your friend gets over. She's experimenting, I guess. She'll straighten out sooner or later.

u really 16? u seem kinda older.

Yep. Don't worry, I'm not some dirty old man trying to perv on you.

good. im ros. ☺

Hi Ros. I'm Jonathan. I'm guessing you just started sixth form too.

yeah. which subjects r u doin?

I rattled them off. There was a pause.

wow. u must b really clever.

I wasn't sure how to answer that, so instead I said, You know what made me laugh? When I got in on Monday college admin had my name down wrong on all the registers. Teachers kept calling me Hawthorn.

hawthorn? that a name?

My middle name – I swear my parents were on crack when they cooked that one up. My dad's a tree surgeon so it must have seemed a good idea. Thank God it's not my first name!

:-P thats funny. im so glad im just rosalind emily.

You got off lightly.

in tree mythology, hawthorns r symbolic of chastity & happiness.

Not sure I like that! You're pulling my leg, right?

no, i just looked it up. i hav sum mythology websites on my faves from when we were doin a project at skool.

Which A levels are you doing? I never asked.

There was another pause. *biology, geography, history,*

art. i like art best. i draw a lot of portraits & things & maybe il go 2 art college later.

Yeah, I saw your art on your profile - really impressive. What other things are you into?

collecting things. bakin cakes. wishin we had a dog.

What do you collect?

china figurines.

I knew the kind she meant. You saw them advertised on the back of TV guides, with a load of tacky garble on how beautifully they're crafted. Freya and I joke that they're only bought by old ladies with no taste.

i also have figurines of characters from sci-fi shows & some animes 2 but there not as easy 2 get as the china 1s.

You into sci-fi?

kinda. lot of its old stuff. no1 at skool really nos wot im talking bout.

Hey, I love old sci-fi! Especially shows that have naff plastic monsters and were patently filmed down a quarry in Dorset. They're hilarious – so not scary.

they r when ur little. i know cos my dad has almost evry episode of dr who eva made & they used 2 give me nightmares.

Man, I wish my dad was that cool! Nearly every episode – seriously?

yup. & star trek. i no the special effects dont stand up now & there kinda tacky but thats partly why i like them.

Exactly! You're so lucky – I keep trying to download episodes but my connection sucks and I can't afford DVDs.

u never said u liked sci-fi on ur profile. it just says u like rock music, computers & horror films & then theres the huge list of bands.

I like to tone the geek thing down.

i dont no much bout music. abby burned me a few cds once but i didnt get into it.

Tell you what, I'll send you some of my favourite tracks. Maybe you'll like them better.

thatd b great ☺ tnx!

No prob. I should warn you, I'm a music nut, so if I go over the top, tell me to shut up.

why rnt u takin music a level then?

Parents.

say no more.

It sucks. If they'd let me apply to the conservatoire (that's a music school BTW) I could have been with Freya.

is freya ur sister ?

Nah, I'm an only child. Freya's my girlfriend and I miss her like crazy.

o. she pretty?

Yeah. Hang on, I'll send you a pic.

Rosalind
8.50 p.m.

As soon as the file transferred, I clicked on it so it filled the screen. A guy and a girl were standing in someone's garden, back to back, smiling at the camera. Both held guitars.

Jonathan's photo reminded me of the trendier sixth-formers at school. He wore baggy jeans with colourful badges stuck all over, a T-shirt with some band logo on, beaded bangles and black-rimmed rectangular glasses, making him look both studious and cool. His long floppy reddish-brown hair was some way between wavy and curly, and for a guy he had big eyes, giving him an earnest look. He was also very skinny, making me wonder if he had some kind of eating disorder.

As for Freya, she was stunning. She had the curves-in-all-the-right-places figure girls dream of and long hair with a thick fringe, the colour of corn. I wondered if it looked as glossy and smooth in real life. Her face reminded me of a figurine's – a red mouth smiling sweetly, small nose, long eyelashes, pink cheeks. And I was fascinated by her outfit. It was too weird not to be retro – a skinny-rib sweater and a skirt that would probably have been called mini back in the sixties, fitted leather boots and lots of colourful jewellery. It should have been a mess, but she pulled it off.

They both looked very grown-up. I was glad I'd lied to

Jonathan about my age. He probably wouldn't have stayed online with a fourteen-year-old, and I really liked talking to him, even if I had to Google some of the things he talked about. I'd had to think fast when he'd asked about my A levels, so I listed the subjects my sister was taking, adding art because it was my favourite.

I realized I hadn't typed a reply for a couple of minutes. I'd been too busy examining the photos. ***yeah shes pretty***, I said.

I'm really lucky. There are way better-looking guys who fancy her.

ur not bad looking. In fact, I really liked the way he looked, especially his smile – genuine, but a little shy. Different from most of the guys I knew, who were all too full of themselves.

That's debatable. I'm definitely not in Freya's league.

guess u have lots in common.

Music, mostly. We do – did – an act with our guitars, writing music and singing. Photo's actually one we used for publicity. Making something and sharing your ideas with someone – that's the best.

i bet. I'd never really shared my drawing with anyone who understood. Abby and people in art class were impressed by my stuff, but they didn't really get it.

So, you've seen me. Do I get to see you?

brb.

I swivelled round in my chair, heart beating quickly.

I hate the way I look. I'm not hideous, but there's nothing about me that would make anyone look twice. Olivia, my sister, has exactly the same eyes and nose and mouth as I do, but on her face they're beautiful. Her hair is a lovely bright brown – mine is mousy and cut like a boy's. She has long eyelashes – I don't. Worst of all, while she has a nice figure, mine has no curves at all. In fact I could be mistaken for a boy. When I wear skirts and jewellery and make-up I look like I'm in drag.

I remember last Christmas when Dad took us up to Nottingham to stay with Gran and Granddad. Olivia and I were both given fifty pounds, and as there wasn't much happening on Boxing Day we went to the shops. It was an agonizing morning. Everything Livy tried on fitted perfectly, whereas I just looked like a kid who'd broken into her mum's wardrobe. I eventually spent most of my money on a figurine. She was wearing a ball gown like the one I graffitied on the wall.

Was it silly that I didn't want Jonathan to know all this? On the Internet I didn't have to be me. I could be whoever I wanted.

I searched through My Pictures for photos and found one taken of Olivia and me this summer in Greece. It showed Livy at her most glamorous in a strappy top and tiny shorts.

I looked childish in combats and a dumb cartoon-character T-shirt.

bak, I said. *sorry, was findin a photo. sendin now. the kid is my sis. shes a pain*.

I awaited his verdict anxiously.

You got all the looks then.

Even though I'd asked for it, I felt crushed.

After we logged off I looked at the photos again, in detail. Jonathan had sent me a few more pictures of Freya – he seemed sickeningly into her. What did she have that made her so attractive to him? OK, she was good-looking, sang and played the guitar and the violin, but what was that special thing? He'd told me they'd been going out for six months. Maybe it was the clothes – not even people in my fashion magazines wore outfits like Freya's. I wondered where she did her shopping – the Internet, maybe.

I switched on my printer, chose the nicest shot of her and ran it off. When the ink was dry I carefully inserted it into a plastic wallet and put it in my ring binder.

Jonathan
9.45 p.m.

I'd just closed the chat window when there was a knock on my door.

'Jonathan, what are you doing in there? Are you all right?'

Why do mothers have to ask such stupid questions? What did she think I was doing, hosting a cabaret? 'Fine. Just mucking about.'

'I thought you'd be out with friends.'

'Obviously not.'

'Can I come in?' Without waiting for an answer, Mum pushed the door open. 'Isn't there anything going on tonight? I'm sure everyone else at college isn't sitting in front of the computer.'

'Nothing I know about.'

She perched on my bed, picking up my pyjamas from the floor and stuffing them under the pillow. 'What happened to the people you used to see on Saturdays?'

'Guess they were more Freya's mates than mine.' I'd seen a few people on the zombie bus and around college, but none had stopped for a catch-up.

Mum frowned. 'Then you need to show them you still want to be friends rather than sitting around waiting for them to contact you.'

'Look, if you must know I was talking to someone online.'

She gave me one of her looks. It was sympathetic, despairing and warning all at once. 'I thought we were past this stage. You know how happy your father and I were when Freya brought you out of your shell. We were worried that all you ever seemed to do was watch things on the computer.'

'Well, maybe life doesn't unfold in neat stages! Last I looked, I wasn't made of assembly blocks and no one wrote any instructions saying how I should be put together.'

'I know Freya's not here now and it's hard doing things by yourself, but you have to try.'

'Maybe I'd feel more like trying if you'd let me go to music school.'

Mum sighed. 'You know why we didn't, Jonathan. It would be very expensive and there'll be plenty of time to study music later, when you have A levels to fall back on.'

'If I'd known this was going to happen, I wouldn't have bothered getting good grades.'

'That's a silly thing to say and you know it.'

'I bet when college is over you'll push me to go to university and tell me music is a waste of time all over again. I heard Dad telling Mr Morrison I was good enough to try for Oxbridge.'

'Your dad gets carried away. It's only because he's so proud. We didn't go to university, so . . .'

'You want me to get the qualifications you didn't. Yeah, figures.'

Mum shook her head. 'The world's very different now, Jonathan. Anyway, you might not have enjoyed music school as much as you think. I'm not sure it would have been the best thing for you – living in London, away from home, having to take out loans to pay your way.'

'Freya would have looked after me.'

'Why don't you see if college has a music club?'

I snorted. 'It'll probably be full of idiots who think Girls Aloud are the pinnacle of modern music.'

'Do you want me to leave you alone?'

I shrugged, glancing at the wall. The mattress made a noise as Mum got up, followed by the creak of a door. I wished she hadn't come in; all she'd done was make me feel angry again. I found myself wondering about Rosalind's parents. She hadn't mentioned them. Despite these wonderful new people I was supposed to have met at college, Ros was the best thing that had happened all week.

Jonathan
Sunday 26 October, 5.30 p.m.

When I left the police station I felt physically sick. Could they really think I'd had something to do with Freya's disappearance – and with those other two girls'? I realized exactly how serious things were when the police rang later that afternoon. They wanted to talk to me again.

The interview took place in the sitting room at home. If that was meant to put me more at ease, it had the opposite effect. Shaw and Turner sat facing me, Mum and Dad on the sofa I usually lay on to watch TV, sipping tea from mugs I used myself. Worst of all were the family photos. When I saw Shaw and Turner looking at the frames on the mantelpiece I felt deeply uncomfortable and, somehow, exposed.

And then the questions started. There were so many I started to become confused.

'We're interested in February's incident, Jonathan. We've had a look through our files but perhaps you'd like to run us through what happened.'

'I don't remember it that well.'

'Really? I find that hard to believe.'

'I don't remember any details. Everything happened quickly.'

'OK, let's go over this. There was an incident with a boy in your year, Tom Copeland. How did it start?'

'He went for me.'

'That's not what his friends said.'

'They were lying! His gang had it in for me.'

'We only have your word on that.'

'It's true – like I said, they lied.'

'Are you sure there wasn't more to this than you're telling us?'

'Of course I'm sure.'

'Was this the first time something like this had happened?'

'Well, I used to take karate, but that's different.'

'Have you ever lost your temper and hit anyone before?'

'No.'

'Positive?'

'I said no!'

'Have you ever hit Freya, Jonathan?'

'What? Of course not!'

'Are you sure?'

'I'd never hurt Freya. I'm not that kind of person.'

'Not even if you lost your temper with her?'

'No!'

'But you're capable of hurting someone. You hurt Tom. Hurt him badly.'

'That has nothing to do with this!'

'What about the night Freya disappeared? You were upset and angry. You've told us that already. Perhaps you couldn't help yourself.'

And on it went. Mum and Dad became angry with all the questions, demanding to know how all this was helping the investigation. I got more and more flustered – and I began to feel guilty too, though I wasn't sure why. It was a relief when Shaw and Turner left. I felt exhausted. If I'd been worried this morning, that was nothing to what I felt now.

Rosalind
Thursday 11 September, 3.35 p.m.

I was getting my sports bag out of my locker at the end of the day when Abby caught up with me.

'Rozzle, can we talk?'

It had been over a week now since I'd put my feelings to Abby. We hadn't exactly fallen out, but things between us had been frosty, and we hadn't met out of school. I'd spent my time at home, mainly chatting to Jonathan. He'd been such good company that I hadn't really missed Abby at all. We talked about old sci-fi and traded links to funny music videos. I'd never had a decent conversation with a guy before, let alone another girl's boyfriend. That bit made me feel a little weird.

'I never wanted things to get like this, Ros,' she said, and I knew she meant it. She'd been caught wearing eyeliner today and had been made to take it off. The smudged circles round her eyes made her look like she'd been crying – and I was pretty certain she had.

'Neither did I,' I said. 'I just wanted to make you feel

bad. I guess that was childish, but you didn't seem to listen to anything I was saying. I was hurt.'

Abby nodded. 'Sorry if I've been ignoring you – I truly didn't mean to. Why don't we just make up? I miss you.'

We hugged each other, and the mood lightened.

'There's another reason I've been rushing to get home. I've been chatting to a boy online.'

Abby's eyes widened. 'Ooh! I want details.'

'His name's Jonathan, and he's just started sixth form. I've talked to him nearly every day since he randomly added me to his contacts list.'

'Wow. What do you chat about?'

'Old sci-fi. Music and art. Pretty much everything really. It's easy to be open with him, maybe because he's more mature than the boys we know, and doesn't just talk about football.'

She was looking impressed. 'Is he fit?'

Picturing him, I nodded.

'You sly thing, Ros. Talking to good-looking boys and not telling me. Are you going to meet up with him?'

'Um, maybe. I mean, it might be hard, as he lives in Norfolk,' I said quickly.

Abby laughed, clapping her hands. 'Ros has a boyfriend!' she crowed. 'You've gone all pink, it must be lurve!'

'Ros has a boyfriend?' Poppy and Kirsten, two girls from our class, came up behind us. Gleefully Abby explained. To my surprise, neither looked too thrilled.

'You realize he's probably not who he says?' Poppy said. 'More likely he's some dirty old man who gets his kicks from picking up teenage girls. You say he just started chatting to you?'

Now I really did go red. 'I know he's genuine. I've seen his photo.'

'That doesn't mean anything,' said Kirsten. 'Even if he sounds like he's sixteen, he could just be pretending.'

'Why do you have to be so mean?' Abby demanded. 'Can't you be happy for Ros?'

Kirsten and Poppy huffed. 'All I'm saying is that you should be careful,' Poppy said. 'And you definitely shouldn't meet up with him if he asks. You can't trust people who hide behind screens.'

Kirsten nodded. 'My mum says it's only girls who don't have the confidence to get real boyfriends who hook up with blokes on the Net.' Kirsten and Poppy moved off, giving me looks that made me feel pathetic, even though I hadn't done anything wrong.

'God!' Abby exclaimed. 'I never knew they were so bitchy! Don't worry, Ros, they're probably just jealous. Neither of them have boyfriends.'

'He's not,' I said in a small voice.

'Not what?'

I opened my mouth – then paused. Abby was never going

to meet him, and she'd sounded so impressed. It wouldn't be a *bad* lie if I pretended Jonathan was my boyfriend. Besides, Abby always had better luck with boys, and it might be nice to feel I had someone to talk about for once.

'Can't remember,' I said airily. 'I'd better get home. I told Jonathan I'd be online.'

The lie sounded so convincing that it surprised me.

Abby nodded. 'OK. Oh, while I remember, I had something to ask you. Ros, I know you don't like Claudia, but on Saturday night we're meeting some blokes she knows at the Malt and Hops. They're artists – you'd be interested in that, right?'

'What kind of artists?'

'I'm not sure, but they've just started a studio. I thought they might be able to give you tips on art colleges and stuff.'

'How does Claudia know them? She doesn't know which way up to hold a paintbrush.'

'She met one of them in a pub. How about it?'

I thought for a moment. If these guys had a studio, they'd be considerably older than us. I could do with their advice and, despite myself, I was intrigued.

3. Be Right Back

Rosalind
5.30 p.m.

I logged on to my account the moment I got in. Jonathan's status was set to 'Away'; probably still getting home from college. I waited impatiently for him to come online. When he did, about half an hour later, I typed, ***good day!*** ☺ ***me & abby made up & we r meetin sum artists on friday.***

Yay! She got the point then?

yeah. tnx 4 all the advice.

Don't mention it. I have news too: FREYA IS COMING TO VISIT ME! I'm working like a maniac to get my homework done before Saturday.

beta stop talkin 2 me then.

You have to stay. I need someone to squee to.

squee?

A squee is a spontaneous expression of delight. SQUEE!

Jonathan continued 'squeeing' about Freya. So much for him being my 'boyfriend'. I wondered what it must feel like to be so into another person.

Jonathan
Saturday 13 September, 12.20 p.m.

I made Dad leave the house fifteen minutes early in case we got stuck in the Norwich traffic and were late for Freya's train. I hovered by the vending machines until I spotted her. She was wearing one of her retro coats and stood out a mile. I tore up the platform.

'It's great to see you,' I said when we broke off kissing. 'You don't know how much I've been looking forward to this.'

There was more I could say, but I remembered that Dad was waiting. Normally I hated it if either of my parents saw me snogging Freya, but today it didn't seem to matter. The important thing was that she was here and we had all day together.

Soon we were heading home, via the chip shop. Dad and Freya, who greeted each other like long-lost friends, started having the conversation they always have when she eats at ours, which usually goes like this:

Dad: Cod? Battered sausages? Steak and kidney pie?

Freya: I'm a vegetarian, Mr O., you know that! You're not going to tempt me over to the dark side any time soon.

Dad: Humans are omnivores, Freya. Our ancestors killed woolly mammoths for a reason. You can't get all your nutrients from tofu.

Freya: But battered sausages aren't real meat. They're all the grimy bits from the abattoir floor, probably much worse than E-numbers. And you should think of the animals: killing cows and pigs – it's no better than murdering babies.

Dad: Large chips for you then?

That's another thing Dad likes about Freya; she has an appetite. He gets very distressed by people who pick at food and moan about waistlines, probably because he's up and down trees all day so he requires hefty meals. He gets almost disturbing satisfaction from watching Freya eat, probably because she doesn't look like someone who has the space to put away second and even third helpings. The truth is that Freya's mother is a health-food freak, meaning Freya's been deprived of what Dad calls 'the good things in life' (fatty meat, huge bowls of pasta and Mum's walnut cake). According to Freya she never tasted chocolate until she had some, aged nine, at a friend's house; like quite a lot of Freya's stories this is probably an exaggeration, but you get the picture.

Mum was as happy as Dad to see Freya, and they immediately started chatting about how her parents were, local gossip, whether living in the city was different to the country, everything. I couldn't wipe a silly grin off my face. For some reason, Freya talking to my parents like another adult made me feel proud.

When the conversation was still going on after lunch

though, I started to get twitchy. Luckily I managed to catch Dad's eye, and he and Mum excused themselves. I made Freya tea (two sugars, no milk) and we took it up to my room. In the early days I always tidied it before Freya came over, but after discovering the state of her room, I stopped bothering. It was nice to feel I could be honest like that.

Freya flopped down on my bed. She picked up my teddy bear from the pillow and pretended to high-five him.

'Hi, Clover! You missed me while I was away in the big bad city, didn't you?' She made Clover wave his arm. 'Yes, Freya, I did,' she growled. 'I missed you ever so much. Jonny's been such bad company since you left, all he does is sit around and pine!'

'Hmmph,' I said, placing the mugs of tea on the floor and sitting next to her. 'Sometimes I think you like Clover best.'

'Cuddly toys have secret lives we don't know about. Fact: Clover told me he's having an affair with the stuffed bunny you gave me.'

'Funny, cos last time I was round yours, that bunny was talking about getting off with your old Barbie dolls.'

'God, such a slut! Clover will be heartbroken!'

'No, he won't, cos his heart is made of foam.'

'Not funny.' But she was giggling, and it felt good to be talking nonsense again. 'Do you realize it's been two weeks and six days since we last saw each other?' I said, putting my arm around her.

'Trust you to count. Hey, you know that girl who disappeared round mine?'

'Oh yeah. Did they find her?'

'Yes, floating in the Thames. Newspapers say she was strangled.'

'Christ. Have they arrested anyone?'

'Not yet. You hear about things like this all the time, but it doesn't feel real; stuff that happens to other people never does. This girl was sixteen, just like me – she could have *been* me, or one of my friends.'

I squeezed her hand. 'Be careful, OK?'

We whiled away the afternoon chatting and playing old CDs we'd made. It was almost like old times, except that Freya hadn't brought her guitar or violin. I tried not to show how disappointed I was. There'd been a melody bothering me all week and I'd been hoping she could help me with it – I never quite got things right when I wrote music alone. But Freya said it sounded too much like schoolwork. Instead she talked, mainly about London and her new friends.

At one point she asked to check her email.

'Someone called Rozzledozzle's messaging you,' she said as she clicked on the Firefox icon.

'Can't think why. Ros *knows* you're here,' I said half-crossly.

'Who's Ros?'

'Girl I met online.'

Freya turned, frowning. Realizing what she was thinking, I said, 'I'm not chatting her up or anything. We just talk every so often. She knows I have a girlfriend – I go on about you all the time.'

'Glad to hear it,' she said pointedly.

At about half six Dad poked his head round the door. 'Shouldn't you two be getting ready?'

'We're going out?' Freya looked startled. 'You never said.'

'That's cos it's a surprise!' I knelt in front of her, taking her hand. 'Freya, would you like to join me for a candlelit dinner at the Market Street Gallery?'

'Seriously? It's really posh there!'

'I know, that's why I chose it. Don't worry, it's on me.'

'He means me,' Dad mouthed, but luckily Freya didn't see. I shooed him away in case he said anything else.

'Is this why you told me to pack something smart?' Freya asked.

'Of course. They don't let any old people in there. And I know you love dressing up.'

She clapped her hands, delighted. 'Are you going to wear a suit?'

'You'll have to wait and see.' I was enjoying this. I'd known it was a good idea; Freya adored surprises. She went to get changed, and I picked up the suit I'd borrowed from Dad. I had to wear my own trousers as Dad's were too short, but the jacket fitted fairly well. More to the point, it made me feel suave. Grown-up. Maybe even a bit James Bondish.

Freya was ages getting ready. When she appeared in a green dress with a huge sticky-out skirt I was lost for words.

'It's fifties style,' she said, giving a twirl. 'Do you like it?'

'You look beautiful.'

'You don't look bad either. Is that actually gel in your hair?'

'Taxi's waiting!' Dad bellowed. Downstairs, Mum insisted on taking photos, and for once I didn't make a fuss. Eventually Dad managed to get us in the van and dropped us off next to the restaurant.

'Wow,' said Freya as he drove off. 'For somewhere so pricey, it's packed, isn't it?'

'Yeah.' I frowned, suddenly uncomfortable.

A very smartly dressed waiter met us at the door.

'Yes?'

I cleared my throat. 'Table for two, please.'

He looked at us down his nose. It was a very long nose, made for sneering. 'Have you made a booking?'

I swallowed. 'Well, no . . .'

'We're fully booked. If sir looks around, he'll see that there isn't a spare table – nor is there likely to be. Perhaps next time sir takes madam out, he might consider making a reservation.'

'But . . .' I struggled to find words. Freya saved me the bother.

'Come on, Jonathan,' she said, pulling me outside. I stared through the window, taking in the candles, the wine glasses, the evening so suddenly ruined.

Freya was looking at me, and I wanted to dissolve to liquid and flow along the pavement, into the gutter and down the drain.

'Mum did tell me to book, but I thought it'd be OK,' I murmured. 'Sorry.'

There was a long silence.

'Maybe we can find somewhere else,' I suggested, but I knew there wasn't much chance of that. We'd be laughed at if we went into any of the pubs, and probably wouldn't be served anyway. The local Indian was a takeaway, and the Chinese had closed down.

We ended up in Bertie's Burger Bar.

'It's not real potato,' Freya said, poking her packet of fries. 'It's all powder, you know. And that milkshake's disguised whale blubber—'

'Look, Freya, I'm sorry, all right? I made a mistake.'

Grinning faces pressed against the window. It was Stuart and his mates. After that there was no peace. They mobbed our table, and Stuart ate all my fries and took the mick out of me for being dressed like I was at a wedding (or a funeral, he said he couldn't tell which). His mates started making lemonade spurt out of their noses and telling dirty jokes, mostly about me and Freya. Then one started getting touchy-feely with her, and when I told him to lay off Freya got the huff and said she could look after herself. By the time Dad came to pick us up I couldn't wait to get home. When we got in I followed Freya straight upstairs to my room.

'Sorry I screwed up,' I said. 'Next time you visit I'll make it up to you.'

Freya shrugged my hand off. 'Maybe next time we won't run into your immature little friends. Have you been bragging about me to them?'

I closed the door, dismayed. 'They're not my mates, OK? I just know Stuart a little. And of course I mention you. You're my girlfriend. You're part of my life.'

'More like some kind of status symbol! You need to make your own mark on people, Jonathan, not use me to impress them.'

'I don't! Well, maybe just a little. When I'm with you I'm someone. On my own I'm just nobody.'

'Of course you're somebody! Don't be silly.'

'I'm not being silly; things have been really tough without you. I love you, Freya.'

'It's like you think we're the same person sometimes,' Freya grumbled. She hunched in my armchair. I knelt by her and took her hand.

'I don't get why you're so mad. Would you rather I pretended I didn't have such a beautiful girlfriend?'

Freya ran a hand over her face, drawing a breath. 'Forget

it, OK? I'm tired and I'm being unfair. 'Night.'

I didn't want go to bed. I wanted to clear the air, ask what I could do to make things better. No, scrap that, I wanted to go back in time and make that table booking and have an amazing romantic evening. Then we wouldn't be in this mess and right now she'd be moaning about having to sleep in the spare room rather than cosying up with me.

Freya gave me a cool peck on the cheek on her way out. I took off my tie and threw it across the room. So much for James bloody Bond.

Ever since we started going out I'd been worried that Freya might lose interest. Even now, I could hardly believe a girl like her had chosen me. While Freya hadn't exactly been one of the 'popular' crowd, she stood out at school because she was beautiful and flaky and did things differently. She was the only kid in the year to use weird organic products in cookery class and she looked tall in school photographs because she wore her thick, waist-length hair piled on top of her head. I used to be fascinated by her hair; however tightly she pinned it up, locks always fought their way out of grips and toggles and by afternoon registration it would be loose.

I'd always had a bit of a crush on Freya, but so did plenty of other guys. Probably I'd never have plucked up the courage to speak to her if she hadn't approached me in music class and asked if I wanted to partner her for our GCSE project.

I could hardly believe my luck. The first time I found one of her hairs stuck to my blazer it made me feel very funny.

To my surprise – and everyone else's – we made a fantastic team. At first there was a bit of friction because my ideas centred around rock music while she was into classical, but this soon proved to be a plus. Freya thought of things I never would have and vice versa. And, in between melodies and quavers, we got to know each other, and before I knew it I had turned into a Freya addict, unable to concentrate on anything else. Problem was, I was still too shy to speak to her outside class. People were always buzzing round her, and I wouldn't have felt comfortable joining them.

It was just as well I discovered that Freya had a Saturday job at an old-fashioned tea shop in one of the neighbouring towns, because waiting for the time between classes to pass was driving me mad. I went to the tea shop the first chance I had. I wore black and brought my guitar, with the idea that I could sit at the back, scribbling music and looking mysterious, as though I was plotting the downfall of the government or something.

I quickly realized it wasn't that kind of tea shop. Everything was decorated in pink and white and the dainty tables made me feel clumsy. The other customers – mostly elderly ladies – stared at my outfit. Worst of all, when Freya appeared I went bright red.

'Hi,' she said, flashing a bright smile. 'Wouldn't have

thought this was your scene.'

I mumbled something lame about fancying tea. She was wearing a dress with a frilly apron that made me feel scruffy. When she brought my tea I drank gingerly, afraid I was going to snap the delicate cup. I couldn't think of anything to say, so left quickly and hung around until the shop closed and Freya came out – almost bumping into me.

'Jonathan! You nearly scared the life out of me. Why are you still here?'

'Waiting for the bus.' That, at least, was true enough. 'Are you going to get it?'

'My dad's picking me up. Want a lift?'

The last thing I felt like was meeting Freya's father, whom I imagined to be the stern, protective sort. So I made up some excuse and got the bus. But I went to the tea shop the next Saturday, and the next, and Freya drifted along to talk to me every so often. She didn't ask why I had suddenly started visiting – it must have been obvious. On the fourth week I even accepted a ride from her dad, who turned out to be about sixty and rather quiet.

One dreadful time I ended up in the tea shop with Mum. She'd forced me to go clothes shopping and we'd spent a ghastly afternoon traipsing round outdated shops.

'I fancy a cup of tea and a cake,' she said. 'Let's go to the Copper Kettle.'

Hastily I said, 'I don't want to. The last time we went

there the cakes were rubbish. I'd rather go home and do my homework.'

She laughed. 'Don't be silly! They do lovely cakes.'

I sat as far back from the table as I could, trying to pretend that Mum was nothing to do with me.

'Hi! What can I get you?' It was Freya, of course, who came to serve us.

'Tea, please,' said Mum.

'Anything to eat? We've got apple turnovers again – the ones you like, Jonathan.'

'Yeah, OK,' I muttered, and Freya went away.

'I thought the cakes were "rubbish" here,' said Mum wryly.

'I only came in here once when I was waiting for the bus.'

'Sure it doesn't have anything to do with our waitress? She's very pretty.'

'She's just a girl from school, OK?'

Mum shut up, but there was a knowing look in her eyes.

On Monday I said to Freya, 'In case you were wondering, I'm not in the habit of hanging out with my mum. Saturday was a one-off.'

'I think it's sweet that you'll go places with her.' Freya tilted her head, smiling. 'You know, you don't have to keep catching me at work. Sundays I'm free all day.'

'Would you like to go somewhere with me next Sunday?'

It was out of my mouth before I had time to think.

'Sure,' she said. 'That'll be great.'

And that was how it started. We went for a walk with our guitars, played a concert to a field of cows, and Freya asked me if I fancied doing a duet in the Easter Cabaret.

'You want me to go on stage with you?' I asked, astonished.

'Why not? You're a fantastic guitarist, and if we're as good at writing lyrics as melodies, it'll be a breeze. I can sing and play rhythm.'

I wasn't sure how I felt about performing in front of the whole school, but I was too awestruck to refuse. 'I never had anyone to share music with before,' I said.

'Me neither.' She smiled. 'So, you going to kiss me now?'

After a few dates she started nudging me to get a better haircut and a cooler pair of specs, and to stop mumbling when I spoke to people. 'There's nothing wrong with you, so be more confident,' she said. My parents had said this before, but coming from Freya I believed it. We worked hard preparing for the concert, and a friend of Freya's took some great publicity photos that we stuck all over school. Now that I was Freya's boyfriend, people started realizing I existed, and it was the happiest time of my life. The concert went amazingly and people were still congratulating us weeks later.

Thinking of the past made me realize how much I missed it. Even though I knew Freya wasn't far away and I could still play my guitar if I wanted, it felt like I'd lost the two things I really cared about. After some minutes of tossing and turning in bed, I knew I wasn't going to sleep, so I got up and logged on to my MyPlace account.

Ros was there. She always was.

Late night hi.

hi. thought u werent going 2 b online 2day.

I shouldn't be but The Worst Night Ever happened.

I told Ros how I'd screwed things up. It was funny how easy I found it to be honest with her; maybe it was because we were chatting over a screen, or perhaps, somehow, I knew Ros wouldn't judge me.

that really is the worst night eva. u must b gutted.

Freya was furious. Says I use her as a status symbol. So what if I do? Aren't I allowed to show off my girlfriend?

maybe shes got used 2 doin things alone. maybe she feels weird bein a couple again.

If it'd been three months since I saw her, maybe, but it hasn't even been three weeks! How can that much have changed?

ur in different places doin different things. maybe u need 2 get 2 no each other all over again.

No, there's something else she's miffed about. Wish she'd tell me. She should, if it's something I can fix.

sumtimes theres no 'should' wiv ppl's feelings – &

maybe u cant solve it either. u expect 2 much of urself.

I raked a hand through my hair. You're probably right. Guess it isn't fair to dump all this on you. You don't even know Freya.

u needed 2 tell sum1. thats ok. il always b here.

What, always? Even when we're old and grey with grandkids?

lol. maybe not like that. u no wot i meant. ☺

Freya and I didn't get much time together on Sunday as she slept in most of the morning. I did go into her room at about ten, but she just pulled the covers over her head. All too soon we were outside her parents' house, saying goodbye. She was spending the afternoon there before going back to London.

'I'll come and visit you soon,' I said, kissing her. 'I really want to see the conservatoire and meet your new friends.'

'Bye.' She picked up her holdall, then dropped it and wound her arms around my neck, squeezing tightly. 'Sorry I've been a bitch.'

did u talk? asked Rosalind when I logged in that evening.

No.

u were the 1 who told me nothin beats honest talkin.

More fool bloody me. Let's not talk about Freya, it's too depressing. How was your weekend?

weird. we met those artists – & i need ur advice.

Rosalind
7.50 p.m.

Abby, Claudia and I arrived at the Malt and Hops early. Despite the chilliness we sat on the benches outside because Claudia said the guys would want to smoke. I was wearing a scarf and hoody with a sweater underneath, and Abby had a coat, but Claudia, in only a strappy top with a push-up bra, denim shorts and tights must have been freezing. I almost felt sorry for her.

I was also wearing a retro hat I'd seen in a charity shop. It was a blue-and-white striped cap, a bit grubby and slightly torn. It covered most of my hair, leaving only a few strands peeking out. Abby fell about laughing when she saw it and asked if I'd lost all sense of style. Maybe it did make me look a little like an old-fashioned schoolboy, but at least it wasn't boring. I'd never had much interest in clothes shopping, but seeing the pictures of Freya had opened my mind and now I felt inspired – perhaps I might be able to get a skirt or top next time, something to give my body a little shape.

The guys were late. Even Abby was starting to mutter about going home by the time three figures appeared at the end of the road. Claudia jumped up, calling out and drawing attention to us, as though the rest of the world cared what we were doing. The man in front greeted her with a kiss on either cheek. He wore an almost too-smart suit and tie and huge gold rings on his fingers. There was no way he was younger than thirty.

'Evening, Clauds, you look great,' he said, sitting next to her. 'How're you doing?'

'Good, now you're here.' Claudia gestured to Abby. 'This is the friend I told you about, Gabe.'

'Hello, darling.' He gave Abby a wave. Then his gaze passed to me. 'I see you brought your kid brother along.'

'Are you joking?' Claudia sniggered. 'That's just someone Abby knows.'

'Rosalind,' said Abby. Her voice sounded the slightest bit shrill. 'She's a girl actually.'

'A cunning disguise. Right.' He laughed. I tried to imagine Gabe holding a paintbrush but couldn't. He looked like I'd imagine an estate agent to.

His friends, whom Claudia introduced as Brian and Hugh, were arguing about whose turn it was to buy the drinks. They looked more like I'd expected: slightly scruffy, in their early twenties.

'I thought they were all meant to be new grads starting up,' I murmured to Abby. 'Gabe's way too old.'

'Maybe he tagged along,' she whispered.

'No way. He's the one Claudia knows; look at them gabbing.'

'What's the secret?' asked Brian, sitting by Abby.

Hugh had gone into the pub.

'Nothing.' Abby managed a smile. 'Oh, I like your earrings.'

'Made them myself.' Brian was skinny, with black hair tied back, a goatee and lots of piercings. The earrings Abby had mentioned were silver and shaped like snakes, with black gems for eyes. His skinny black jeans and the skull-shaped buckle on his belt – very like one Abby owned – suggested that he fancied himself as a goth.

Pointedly I said, 'Claudia told us you were artists. You don't look like it.'

Gabe grinned. 'What d'you think an artist looks like? Flowing hair and a beret? Sure we're artists. We have a great studio.' His arm snaked round Claudia's shoulders. She shot me a superior look.

'I've been there. Gabe's going to be a big photographer one day.'

'Really,' I said. 'What does he photograph?'

'Lots of stuff,' Gabe said, stroking Claudia's hair. 'You've seen some of my snaps, right, babe?'

'They're amazing.' Claudia was practically purring.

Like you'd be able to tell, I thought.

Hugh came out from the pub holding a tray. On it were three pints, two halves of cider – and a Coke. He winked as he took the space opposite me.

'You're too cute to get drunk, kid.'

I opened my mouth to say that I was the same age as Abby and only one year younger than Claudia. Then I received a sharp kick under the table that made me bite my lip in pain. Claudia was glaring at me, and I began to understand. I pushed my Coke to one side.

'Abby,' I whispered, 'leave that cider. It might be spiked. I don't like these guys.'

But Abby's attention was on Brian.

'You actually sell jewellery at Camden Market? That's so cool!'

'Come over sometime and I'll show you what I've got,' Brian said.

I looked over the other side of the table. Claudia was cosied up to Gabe and sampling his pint, seemingly enthralled by his words.

'. . . I'm thinking of blowing up a couple of snaps I've had hanging round the studio and selling them to art galleries. They'd be worth a bit.'

In your dreams, I thought. I knew that art was difficult to make a living out of. If Gabe thought he could be successful without breaking into a sweat, he was mad, or lying – probably both.

'Looks like it's you and me,' chuckled Hugh. Was this some kind of weird triple date? I wondered, turning my attention to him. Here was someone whose portrait I wouldn't mind drawing; Hugh had good bone structure, with a strong, straight nose and high cheekbones. His dark hair needed a cut and it didn't look as though he'd shaved for a couple of days, but if he brushed up a bit I'd definitely call him handsome.

'Not drinking your Coke?' he asked. 'Promise I didn't spike it.'

'That's what all drink dopers tell their victims,' I said. 'Anyway, the coke here is always flat.'

'Oh, you're a regular. At such a tender age.'

'I didn't choose to come here.' I nodded at Claudia. 'It's her hang-out.'

'From what I hear, she's in and out all the pubs in London,' said Hugh. 'The George in Kensington is where Graham met her.'

'Graham?'

Hugh grinned. 'You didn't really think his name was Gabriel, did you?'

I glanced at Gabe. He was laughing again and smoking something that didn't smell like a normal cigarette. 'He's way too old for Claudia.'

'Who cares?' Hugh took a red paper packet out of his pocket. 'Fancy a doughnut? Bought a pack from Tesco on the way here and there's two left. Bit squashed, but perfectly edible.'

He held one in front of me. It was the cheap, sugar-coated type I adored. I looked at it longingly then shook my head. 'No, thanks.'

'Go on. You know you want to.'

'What don't you understand about the word "no"?'

'Ouch! It bites back.' Hugh sank his teeth into a doughnut. 'Your loss, Miss Way-Too-Suspicious.'

'Hey, Ros!' Abby sounded excited. 'Did you hear what Gabe said?'

'She was too busy dissing my doughnuts,' said Hugh. '*Répétez, s'il vous plaît.*'

'We should meet up round our place sometime and hang out.' Gabe waved a hand round the table with the air of a preacher addressing a large audience. 'I promised Clauds I'd show her the studio properly.'

'All of us?' Abby's eyes lit up.

Brian tugged her ponytail. 'Sure. Why not?'

'Whatever,' Gabe said, sounding bored. 'We're cool with anything. Now will someone get me another pint?'

At about half ten the guys suggested moving on to a bar, but Abby and I knew our parents expected us home. Though I could get away with sneaking in late, Abby's mum and dad usually waited up. If they had their way, she'd be home by ten; it was only because I was allowed out an hour later that they'd extended her curfew to eleven. It was our good luck that we lived down the same well-lit street.

As Abby was saying goodbye, Claudia took my arm and

dragged me away from the others. Leaning close, she hissed, 'Gabe and the others think Abby's sixteen and I'm eighteen. You rat on us, I'll make your life hell. Got it?'

'Got it,' I mumbled. Claudia let go of my arm, giving me one of her superior, catty smiles.

'That was fun,' Abby said when we were round the corner. 'I was as freaked out as you at first, but they're nice, aren't they?'

'I guess, but don't you think it's strange they want to hang out with us? Don't they have girlfriends their own age?'

'Brian and Hugh are only twenty-two. Didn't you like them?'

I shrugged. Those two weren't so bad, but Gabe gave me the creeps. His vague, all-too-easy manner bothered me. I got the same feeling around him that I did with Claudia: something beneath the surface wasn't right.

'Didn't you think Gabe was weird?' I asked.

Abby wrinkled her nose. 'He was OK, but I don't get why he's mates with the other two.'

'Maybe they're not mates.' In fact, I'd got the impression Hugh and Brian were cautious around him. Though Gabe seemed to be the one paying for all the drinks, it had been the other two who'd been collecting them from the bar. At one point, Hugh had grumbled that he wasn't Gabe's servant. Gabe had just laughed and given Hugh a tenner and a push that was a bit too forceful to be friendly. 'So is Claudia going out with him?'

'Kind of. They've met up a few times, and she's stayed over at his.'

'She's not sleeping with him, is she?'

'Dunno,' said Abby. Then, more defiantly, 'So what if she is? It's not a big deal – just like us going to their place next weekend isn't a big deal.'

'That's only what they *said*.'

'They want us to come over, and why not? We're not kids. My parents wouldn't approve, but I don't care. Brian and the others are fun – exciting – different. And Claudia's up for it.'

I wanted to argue, but I hesitated, and Abby noticed.

'Ros, relax. I don't get you – you won't trust people we've just had a nice evening with, and yet you tell your Internet boyfriend everything.'

'Yeah, but Jonathan's not like these guys.'

'You don't even know who he is! Poppy and Kirsten might be right – it's dead dodgy getting that close to someone on the Net.'

'Well, maybe I am playing a dangerous game,' I snapped, 'but it's no more dangerous than what *you're* doing. These guys probably just want sex!'

'How do you know that's not what Jonathan wants?'

'I just do, OK!'

'Just like *I* know Brian and the others are nice guys!'

We glared at each other and there was a moment of silence. Then Abby said, 'I don't want to fall out again, Ros. It's fine for you to be all snooty – you already have someone, but I don't, and I really like Brian. I'm going to the studio next weekend – and it'll be more fun if you come too. That's all.'

What could I say? I'd feel terrible staying home while Abby was in the centre of London with Claudia and three guys we hardly knew. Despite being sure it was a bad idea, I found myself saying yes.

im not stupid 4 worrying, am i? I asked Jonathan. ***older guys who hang round girls usually just want 2 sleep wiv them.***

Weird they didn't want to take your picture. You're really pretty.

I was glad neither of us had webcams. *You're a liar, Ros Fielding*, I thought. Pretending that Jonathan was my boyfriend was easy. I saved our conversations, and every so often I looked at his photo and wondered what his voice sounded like and how it might feel if he kissed me. It had been little things at first – seeing a guitar and imagining him doing his act. These days I couldn't pass a couple in the street without wondering about Jonathan and Freya – all kinds of stuff, like how much she loved him and whether they'd slept together. Pretending that Olivia was me though – that was a lie I wished I didn't have to live. The more we spoke, the more I wanted him to like me for being Rosalind, not the pretty girl in the photo.

wot do i do? I asked. *abby & me hav been friends since we were 7. we stick together.*

Funny how sometimes friendship makes you go against your natural instincts. Let someone you trust know where you are. Your sister, if you don't want your dad to know.

dad isnt round enough 2 notice if im there or not.

Tell you what. Let me know the address of this studio. I'll give you my number. If anything goes wrong, miscall me. I promise I'll contact the police.

wd u do that 4 me?

Sure. Here it is. Actually, here's my home one too, just in case.

& heres mine. tnx 4 talkin this thru wiv me.

No prob. Hey, we should meet up sometime.

I swear I stopped breathing.

I'm planning to visit Freya on the weekend of 27th/28th – it's her birthday on the 30th and I want to hand over her present. I could meet you on the Saturday for lunch or something.

Oh God! I thought. What do I do? He thinks I'm Olivia! And this was the very thing I'd been warned about – meeting strange people off the Net.

Only if you want to.

My fingers fluttered over the keyboard.

Still there?

of course i want 2 meet up!

Cool. You can meet my train.

yeah. ok. great.

I swivelled round in my chair to face the wall, feeling like my stomach had left my body.

4. Invisible

Rosalind

Friday 26 September, 6.20 p.m.

I spent the week fretting, only to hear that the aren't-artists (as I had dubbed them in my head) had blown us out.

'Claudia says they're busy this weekend,' Abby told me. 'Next Friday's cool though.'

Brilliant – now I would have to worry all next week too. I hoped they would cancel again.

But before I could blink, Friday had come. Time works in funny ways, I thought as I checked that I had enough cash for the tube. Drags when you want it gone, and shoots forward when you don't.

'Enjoy the cinema.' Dad appeared at my bedroom door. 'Petra and I are trying that Turkish restaurant tonight – dining like sultans.'

'Have fun.'

Dad paused. 'Is there anything worrying you, Rozzle?'

'No,' I lied. 'Why would there be?'

'You were up late typing. I heard keys clicking. Are you behind on schoolwork?'

''Course not.'

'What were you doing then?'

Dad is very laid-back, but occasionally he has fits of conscience and starts interfering. 'I was talking to a friend.'

'Abby?'

'No. Someone I met online.'

Dad frowned, and I wanted to smack myself for being so stupid. 'Not sure I like you talking to strangers. There are a lot of weirdos out there.'

I started edging towards the door.

'I mean it. Sick old guys posing as teenagers.'

'Yeah.' I squeezed past him. 'See you later.'

'Rozzle, wait. I want to know how you started talking to this person.'

I closed my eyes a second, thinking that even visiting the aren't-artists had to be better than an interrogation. 'He messaged me on MyPlace.'

'Oh, *he* did, did he? What were you talking about?'

'Just stuff.'

'Can you promise it was nothing that would worry me?'

My father and I have different ideas of what's worrying, so I dodged that question. 'He's not a dirty old man, if that's what you're thinking. He's sixteen.'

'So he says. Be careful, Ros.'

'I am,' I snapped. 'It's not a big deal.'

'Yes, it is – you're still a kid, and this is serious. Has he asked you to meet him?'

'No.'

'He has, hasn't he?'

'I said no!'

Olivia's door opened. 'What's all the yelling about?' she asked.

'Rosalind's been speaking to strange men online.' said Dad. 'She doesn't seem to realize how dangerous it is.'

'Freak,' said Olivia.

I ignored her and turned to Dad, trying to keep my temper.

'All I'm saying is not everyone you meet on the Internet is dodgy.'

'Of course not – but they could be. Look, Rosalind, I don't like thinking the worst of people before I've met them, but too many vulnerable kids have been preyed on over the Internet for me to let this go. Do you understand what I'm saying? I worry about you sometimes.'

I didn't answer. Olivia snorted, and I rounded on her. 'If you want someone to worry about, try Livy! She's the one who came back at half one last weekend from a date with Mr Wonderful.'

'Sneak! You're just jealous because no one would ever want to date you.'

'That's enough!' Dad rarely raises his voice, so we shut up, Olivia giving me a furious look as I escaped downstairs.

'We'll talk more about this later,' Dad shouted after me. 'Make sure you're back by eleven!'

'Gladly!' I muttered under my breath.

★

The entire journey I felt like I wanted to throw up. Abby sat chatting to Claudia on the other side of the carriage, wearing her best jewellery and fully gothed out in a beautiful lace shirt over a black strappy dress. Claudia was her usual tarty self in yet another titchy outfit. This time I hoped she really did get cold. I hadn't bothered to dress up, though I was wearing my retro cap. There was no way I could compete, and the less attention I got the better.

Another problem was our eleven o'clock curfew. If I counted walking from home to the station, the journey was an hour and twenty minutes, plus the time it would take us to walk to Gabe's. I'd told Abby we'd have to leave at half nine, but I wasn't sure she'd been listening. Dad would probably be back late, but I couldn't bank on that, and he'd hit the roof if he found out I'd lied to him.

At least Jonathan was on my side. Somehow that didn't feel as comforting as it ought to. Though I'd been defiant with Dad, his words had struck a nerve – because despite myself, there had been moments I'd wondered if I was right to place so much trust in Jonathan. After all, his first message had just appeared on my screen. Me, out of billions of Internet users. And he'd changed me. I'd never been the kind of girl who fell for people quickly, but I'd certainly fallen for him. Had that just happened – or had Jonathan encouraged me? Nothing had been said directly, but I couldn't help remembering how he'd asked to see my photo. He hadn't exactly hidden how pretty he thought Olivia was either. Sick old guys who targeted teenagers would know how to draw girls in without it seeming obvious . . .

Oh, shut up! I thought, angry with myself. All I seemed to do was worry these days – I wished I could lighten up.

When we got out at High Street Kensington, my phone vibrated. The text was from Jonathan: **Remember to miscall me and I will fly to your rescue ☺ I've got the address on a Post-it.**

'This area's classy,' Abby said as we stepped through the station barriers. It had upmarket coffee shops and trendy clothes stores – exactly what you'd expect to find on a well-to-do high street. I assumed we'd be led down a grubby alleyway, but Claudia took us to a respectable-looking road with tall terraced houses, the five-storey kind that have basement entrances. Gabe's was tattier than the others, but I had no doubt that it was worth a small fortune. Perhaps I'd been wrong about him after all.

'Hi, girls.' Gabe answered the door, yet again in shirt and tie. 'Great to see you; come on in.'

I gave the street a last look then stepped inside. The hall was bare, with faded patches on the old-fashioned wallpaper where paintings might once have hung, and there was a naked bulb dangling from the ceiling. The staircase creaked as we made our way to the next floor and into a big room with long windows. It was sparsely furnished, with empty takeaway cartons and dirty cutlery on the floor. Brian and Hugh were sprawled across a sofa watching TV. Between them sat a grubby-looking Jack Russell. Seeing us, he jumped off the sofa and started barking, wagging his stubby tail.

'Will someone shut that animal up?' Gabe levelled a kick at the dog, who dodged and retreated behind the television. He did, however, stop yapping.

Hugh and Brian shuffled up to make room for Abby, and Claudia spread out on the second sofa with Gabe. Seeing no other seats, I hovered where I was.

Hugh gave me a wave. 'Hey, Ros. You don't have to stand. There's a beanbag over there.'

I picked up the beanbag and pulled it up by Abby, settling down gingerly.

'Great house, isn't it?' said Gabe. 'Used to be an upstairs-downstairs kind of place, servants and all. It's so large that there are rooms up top I haven't even found uses for yet! All mine too.'

'Don't you three share?' Abby asked.

'Nah, the guys are just human furniture. Get us some drinks, will you, Bri?'

Brian went out of the door grumbling and returned with a pack of beer cans and a bottle of vodka. Gabe opened the vodka and gave it to Claudia, who acted as though he'd given her the most amazing present. When the bottle got to Abby, she looked at it doubtfully, but took a long swig, probably not wanting to look a kid. I tried a sip, grimacing at the strong burning taste, and quickly passed it on.

'A bit more relaxed now, girls?' asked Gabe, rolling a cigarette. 'Having a good time?'

'Um, yeah. Thanks.' Abby gave a little giggle. 'It's really cool here.'

'The kid doesn't look happy.' I realized he was looking at me. 'What's wrong with her? Doesn't like strange men?'

'She doesn't like anything,' said Claudia. I glared at them both.

Gabe started chuckling. 'God, if looks could kill! Kid gives me the creeps.'

'The feeling's mutual,' I snapped.

His chuckle turned to laughter. 'Here, this'll lighten her up; take this, darling. Want me to show you how it's done?'

He passed the joint in my direction.

'I don't smoke,' I said.

'Ah, but this isn't a cigarette. It's something special – good stuff.'

'I know what it is and I don't want it,' I said, hunching my shoulders and wishing I wasn't there. Luckily Hugh chose that moment to flip on a CD of eighties hits. Gabe forgot about me and offered the joint to Claudia, and Abby started chatting to Brian. Hugh picked up a beer can.

'You don't want to be here, do you?' he said.

'Someone noticed,' I muttered.

'Look, Ros, you may as well try to enjoy yourself rather than sit there sulking. Your mate said you were into art; want to have a look at our photos?'

Couldn't hurt, I supposed. 'Sure.'

I followed Hugh into the next room. He perched on a table and took out an A3 file, opening it at a shot of a sunset-bathed beach. I flicked through the pages, taking in a busy Spanish street, beauty spots from across the world and shoots with models. My favourite showed a colourful houseboat docked at the side of a river. Its nameplate, which read *Annabel*, had two mermaids painted either side of it. A white greyhound was lying on the roof, sunbathing.

'These are good,' I said. 'Did you take them?'

'Yup. The boat's my dad's; it's moored at Little Venice.' Seeing my blank expression, Hugh said, 'The canal near Maida Vale – he's been living there for years.'

'Oh. Did you grow up on a boat then?'

He laughed. 'Hell, no! I only go there for the odd weekend; his mind's off with the fairies, my dad. Here, let me show you some of Graham's.'

There was another folder on the table. I opened it. These photos were dull by comparison, and looked very amateurish.

I saw that Hugh was grinning. 'Crap, aren't they?'

I nodded. 'I thought this was supposed to be a studio.'

'Fat chance; Graham's mental. He's just a poser who thinks he can play at being in business. Got ideas after his aunt popped her clogs and left him this place.'

'So you're not mates then?'

'Graham's a pain in the arse.' He lit a cigarette. 'I'd move out tomorrow if I had any cash, but he doesn't charge rent and that's too good to pass up. Your friend's making a big mistake with him.'

'Claudia's not my friend,' I said, 'but he's far too old for her.'

'It's not just that. Want me to tell you a story?' Without waiting for my reply, Hugh carried on, 'I met Brian at college when I was finishing off my photography MA. Both of us had itchy feet; he was cut up about his long-term girlfriend dumping him, and I didn't fancy getting a job straight after graduation – so we decided to go backpacking round Europe.'

'What's an MA?'

'Master of Arts – extra year after a regular degree. Anyway, I decide I'm going to use the time abroad to build up a really decent portfolio so someone might actually want to employ me. For a while everything's peachy. Then we hit Paris. Ever been there?'

I shook my head.

'You'd like it – lots of art galleries. Anyway, I've got a great angle on the Eiffel Tower when this bloke trips over me – he's been walking backwards looking through his camera. He apologizes and we joke about it and get talking.' Hugh shook his head. 'Paris, the most romantic city in the world, and I meet Graham there. You couldn't make it up.'

'What happened next?'

'We have a drink and a laugh. He's looking for a place to stay so Bri and I take him to our hostel. Turns out he's on a photography tour too, financed by a wealthy aunt who was fond of him as a kid, only he's pissed the money up the wall and is trying to get by on a shoestring till it's time to go home. Starts sponging off us the moment he can, the bastard.'

'Starting to see why you don't like him now,' I said.

'The real crunch comes a few nights later,' said Hugh. 'I come back to the hostel to find that someone's been through my stuff. See, I've been storing my photographs on memory cards and copying them on to my laptop, only the piece of junk hasn't been working properly, so not all my stuff's backed up. And guess what, the memory cards have been nicked. Three weeks' work gone, just like that!'

He paused to take a drag on his cigarette. 'I had it out with Graham right away. He denied it – said he was in his room with a headache – total shit. I reckon he knew he was a crap photographer and was panicking about having something to take back to dear old auntie, who's arty and knows how to tell good from bad. Want to hear the best bit?'

'I think you're going to tell me anyway.'

Hugh laughed. 'Sorry, am I boring you? Graham's a bad subject to get me going on. Anyway, he gets it into his head to pin everything on these two Polish girls in the next room, probably cos they're easy targets. So we have this ridiculous showdown, with him going on at them, while all the time I know he did it. We nearly got chucked out of the hostel.'

'Did you find the memory cards?'

'No; Graham didn't have them on him. But I know he nicked them, cos when we got home he entered my shots into a competition.' He shook his head. 'Won a thousand quid I could really have done with. It sucks.'

'Didn't you say anything?'

'Got no proof, have I? We were both hanging out in Paris, taking photos of the same things. It's my word against his.'

Hugh finished his cigarette. I wasn't quite sure what to say. I wondered if these guys thought Claudia, Abby and me were 'easy targets' too. I shook my head when Hugh offered me his beer can.

'No, thanks. I'm too cute to get drunk.'

He rolled his eyes. 'You know what you are, Ros? Uppity. And, if I'm not mistaken, just the slightest bit bitter.'

I folded my hands behind my back, a little embarrassed. 'I'm not uppity. I just like to know where I am and right now, I don't.'

'Nah, you've got issues. Parents smack you about or something?'

I wasn't sure if he was teasing or not. 'My mum walked out on us. Does that count?'

My pocket vibrated and I took my phone out. Jonathan had texted me: **OK?**

I quickly replied: **think so.**

'Boyfriend?' asked Hugh.

'What makes you think that?'

He pointed to my cheeks. 'Gone pink. I'm happy for you.'

'What do you mean?'

'I was beginning to think you were a total killjoy.' He winked. 'Whether you're afraid of being hurt, or protecting yourself, whatever, way too controlled isn't healthy.'

Thinking of the lies I'd told Jonathan, I said, 'If anything, I'm out of control. I've dug myself into a hole I can't get out of.'

'Long as it's not a hole a coffin goes in, you'll get by.' With the air of a philosopher, Hugh said, 'Love's good when it's there, crap when it screws you over, but what it does do is tell you who you are – that's what I say.'

I was spared replying by the entry of the Jack Russell. Dropping down on to my knees, I offered him my hand.

The dog sniffed at it, then butted his head against my leg. Despite myself, I giggled.

'Is he your dog?'

'He's no one's dog,' said Hugh. 'Found him outside the house about two months ago and gave him a doughnut. Next morning he was still there, and somewhere along the line he ended up staying. Good job he's got comedy value, cos he's an ugly mutt.'

I had to agree. The dog's coat was mucky white and he had a scar across his muzzle and the end of one ear was missing.

'What's his name?'

Hugh shrugged. 'We just call him Dog.'

So no one cared about him either. I scratched Dog behind the ears.

'I've always wanted a dog,' I said. 'But my dad says it would be too much work.'

'Then you need a guttersnipe like this one. Dog isn't any work at all; even takes himself for walks if you let him out, and he's more than happy to eat takeaway leftovers.'

'Is it healthy to be feeding a dog McDonald's?'

'Hey, even we don't feed the dog that crap! No, his favourite is chicken in satay sauce.'

Through the gap in the door I saw that Abby and Brian were on their feet.

'Better join my friend,' I said. 'Thanks for showing me the pics.'

Hugh waved. 'See you later.'

I caught up with Abby going up the stairs to the third floor. I saw another dusty staircase leading further up – Gabe hadn't been exaggerating when he'd said the house was huge. Abby was in a giggly mood and I wished I felt comfortable enough to join in. We spent an hour or so looking at Brian's jewellery. It was interesting at first, but soon the necklaces started blurring into one, and Brian kept droning on in far too much detail about how he'd made each piece. I could also tell that he was itching to get rid of me, but I wasn't sure whether Abby wanted me there or not. So I hung about, feeling awkward and more and more aware that time was marching on. When it neared half nine, I said in a small voice, 'Abby, we should go.'

Abby made a face. 'Ros is saying we need to head out,' she said to Brian. 'It's just this really stupid curfew our parents have.'

'Do you want to leave?'

Abby shook her head until her dangly earrings danced. 'No, I mean, I'm having a really good time.'

'Don't then,' Brian said, as though it was as simple as that.

Alarmed, I grabbed Abby's arm. 'Your mum and dad get twitchy if you're even five minutes late, remember?'

She glanced at me, then at Brian. He shrugged, looking bored, and went out of the room.

'Thanks for that,' said Abby, staring after him. 'Now he

thinks I'm a stupid little kid. So will Claudia.'

'Your parents will freak – you know they will.'

'Not if I tell them I'm staying over at yours.' She took out her mobile. 'They think I'm at your house anyway. We could just stay a little longer, then get back ages before your dad comes home.'

'What if he's back early? What if your parents mention it to him sometime?'

'Oh, stop being so boring, Ros! Go, if you so desperately want to. I'll make my own way home.'

'You know I can't do that. I don't trust these guys or Claudia anywhere near enough to leave you.'

'What exactly do you think they're planning, for God's sake? If they were going to murder us, don't you think they'd have done it by now?'

For a moment I wondered if I was being way too suspicious, like Hugh had said. 'Do you really like Brian this much?' I asked.

Abby fiddled with her necklace, not replying instantly. 'Well, yeah. And I bet if this was *Jonathan*'s house you'd be lying to your parents too.'

This made me feel guilty. She had a point.

'OK, we'll stay,' I mumbled. 'Like, half an hour. No more.'

'Yeah. Half an hour, just so they don't think we're really uncool. Then I promise you we'll go.'

Jonathan
9.00 p.m.

Think so – not the most informative text, but at least it told me Ros was still in one piece. So I settled down to watching 'The Caves of Androzani' on my computer. I was excited about 'Androzani'; according to everything I'd read on the Internet, it was one of the best *Doctor Who* serials ever made. When I'd mentioned this to Ros, I hadn't been expecting her to post me her dad's copy, along with several other DVDs. The package had arrived this morning, complete with a note.

Hi Jono,
what's up? I thought I'd send you a surprise as I know you had a pants week at college. I hope these are ok. Don't think you have seen them and I know you were keen on androzani. If you have, then I guess I can always lend you some more and maybe some Star Trek too. Let me know what you think of them anyway.
Ros x

The notepaper was lilac, with a fancy border, and she'd doodled a few Daleks at the bottom, which made me smile. When I turned the note over I found a couple of crumbs stuck to the back. Maybe they were from one of the cakes she liked baking. Though we chatted almost every day, somehow the note brought Ros to life in a way the computer screen couldn't.

I was halfway through the second episode when there was a knock on my door.

'Jonathan?'

I quickly paused the DVD and minimized the player. Mum came in, a cup of tea in her hand.

'Thought you might like a drink,' she said, putting it on my desk.

'Thanks.' I waited for Mum to go, but instead she moved round my room, flicking dust off the shelves.

'Have you and Freya got plans for the weekend?'

I made a non-committal noise. 'Probably go round the conservatoire. Meet her new mates.'

'Good.' Mum had a concerned expression on her face that instantly annoyed me. 'You've spent too much time on your own recently.'

'Yeah, well, there's no one at college I particularly fancy speaking to.'

'What about Lucy? She seems nice. Always says hello when we drop you off at the bus stop.'

I groaned, raising my eyes to the ceiling.

Mum frowned. 'I'm serious. You've been at college weeks now. I would've thought you'd have made friends, or at least kept up with your old ones.'

'I told you before, Mum, most of the people I hung out with were Freya's friends. Yeah, they were OK, but now she's not here, we don't seem to have much in common.'

'Jonathan –' Mum's low tone of voice hinted that her patience was running thin – 'you're not even trying, are you?'

'I am! You just assume I'm not because you've got this thing about me being socially retarded. God's sake, Mum, you seem to think making friends and fitting in is easy. Here's some news: it isn't!'

'Please don't get worked up. I didn't come in to upset you.'

'Well, you are! And you know what? This is your fault!'

Mum stared at me. 'What on earth do you mean?'

'You know exactly what I mean.' I knew I was getting into dangerous territory, but I couldn't stop myself. 'You're the one who made me go to that college, do four subjects I don't care about, refused to listen when I told you it wasn't what I wanted.'

'Jonathan, we discussed why we didn't want you to go to music school at the time.'

'We never discussed anything; you just told me I couldn't! You wouldn't even let me do music A level – so now I'm stuck taking further maths instead, despite it being totally redundant.'

'You don't seem to realize how special you are, or what a bright future you have. You got full marks in physics and maths! That doesn't happen to many kids. To throw that away because . . . just because you've had fun doing your music act with Freya—'

'Did you hear us play, Mum? We were great – more than great! Everyone said so. That doesn't happen to *many kids*, either!'

'Of course you were good, I know that. But a musical career, Jonathan – you can do better. With the A levels you're taking you'd be able to go into medicine . . . engineering . . .'

If I felt angry before, now I was furious. 'Who are you to tell me I can do better? All I was asking was to do one A level I wanted, Mum, one crappy A level out of four, but no, I couldn't even have that. How can I make you understand – music isn't some passing phase. It's my life, and you've no right to take that away from me.'

'You still have your private music lessons—'

'*Freya*'s parents let her go to the conservatoire – *they* respect her wishes. What if she gets so much better than me that I can't keep up? What if she finds someone else in London while I'm not there?'

'What's going on?' Dad appeared in the doorway.

'A levels again.' Mum sighed. 'Jonathan seems to think we've ruined his life—'

'Well, you have!' I yelled. 'I'm never enough for you, am I? I always have to be more – always have to be pushed to be better than everyone else – you just can't accept me as I am. Well, swallow this – I'm miserable, I hate college, I hate everyone there and right now I hate being me. So thanks, Mum, thanks, Dad – I hope you're happy now.'

'That's not fair . . .'

'I knew you'd argue – you never listen to me. Well, know what? I don't want to listen to you, so you can get out of my room and leave me in peace!'

Mum opened her mouth, then closed it. She looked at Dad, who shrugged.

'All right,' she said in a tight voice. 'If you want to talk about this calmly, we're downstairs.'

I turned my back on them, and after a moment heard the door close. Once I was sure they were out of hearing distance I took out my anger on the furniture, slamming fists and feet into my table, the bed and against the wall. I only stopped when my chair dipped to one side, one leg snapped. Oh, crap! I thought, kneeling down to check the damage. It worried me when I flipped like this – I didn't like to think of myself as aggressive, but the chair wasn't the first thing I'd broken.

I didn't feel like watching *Doctor Who* any more. I flopped on my bed, staring at my CDs and my guitar and wondering how on earth Mum and Dad's A-level reasoning could ever have made any sense to me. I couldn't wait to get out of the house and see Freya and Ros. I felt sure they'd understand.

Thinking of Ros reminded me I'd promised to be on call for her. I picked up my phone. A new text awaited me.

got problem. abby doesnt want 2 leave.

Rosalind
9.40 p.m.

After Abby had called home we went downstairs. The room stank of weed and a black-and-white comedy show was blaring from the TV. The only person watching it seemed to be Hugh, who was eating jam straight from the jar. Gabe and Claudia were stretched out on one of the couches snogging, and Brian was leaning against the wall with a fresh beer.

'Going home?' he asked.

'No,' Abby said after a pause.

'Great; I was hoping you'd stay.' Brian settled on Hugh's couch, patting the seat next to him. Abby stared at it, then glanced at Claudia. Very slowly she went over and sat down. I moved to the window, wishing I'd never been stupid enough to come here. For a moment I was tempted to head out and chance the journey, but I didn't know this part of

London and I was a little afraid of walking through the dark streets on my own. Hadn't Jonathan said that a girl from Freya's area had been snatched off the street and killed?

Minutes dribbled by. I dragged my beanbag to the window and turned my back on the room, making it very clear I wasn't interested in what everyone else was doing. Dog appeared, head in a takeaway carton that he had pushed round the room. Realizing he was trying to lick it out, I held it still. By the time Dog was finished, orange sauce was speckled all over his muzzle.

'Hugh was right; you are a guttersnipe,' I muttered, and did my best to clean him up with the end of my sleeve.

As soon as my watch showed ten, I got up, thankful that this horrific evening was almost over – and saw Abby snuggled up to Brian. He was stroking her hair, saying something I couldn't catch, and she seemed to be drinking it in. I began to feel a little panicked – there was no way she'd want to go now. What should I do? Maybe Jonathan would know.

I went up and tapped Hugh on the shoulder.

'Could I use your Internet?'

He looked amused. 'The days when I got decent Internet are long gone, I'm afraid. My piece-of-junk laptop's in an advanced stage of dying. You're better off trying the cafe at the end of the road – stays open till two.'

It was a good job I had Jonathan's number, I thought,

slumping down on the beanbag. Right now I didn't care if Jonathan was who he said or not, I needed to talk to someone I trusted.

He replied to my text a few minutes later: Can't you go home alone?

no. dangerous + dont want 2 leave abby.

Want me to call you?

no dont want them 2 overhear. dad out 2nite shouldnt no im late but still worried. will hav 2 catch last train.

'Get the feeling we're the odd ones out?'

I looked up at Hugh, then across the room. Gabe and Claudia were still snogging, and now Abby and Brian had started too.

'That's nothing new,' I muttered.

'Why don't you come and sit over here with me?'

I stiffened. 'What?'

'Promise I don't bite.'

'No, thanks.'

For a moment Hugh looked confused, then he laughed. 'Oh Christ, you think I'm trying to hit on you. Well, sorry to disappoint, Ros, but I'm not interested in kids. Nothing personal. All I meant was you might like to bring that beanbag somewhere you can see the telly.'

Cheeks red and not looking at Hugh, I shuffled into a better position. I didn't like how amusing he seemed to find me, but at least he wasn't ignoring me like everyone else was. I was beginning to feel like my beanbag was a tiny island in a sea of coupleyness. It was just as well that the television volume was loud enough to drown the sounds from the sofa.

I tried to watch the comedy show, which seemed to be going on forever, but I didn't get any of the jokes. Every time Hugh laughed, I jumped. It began to feel like I was trapped in a very weird nightmare.

At least Dog provided a distraction. He started sniffing at some fresh takeaway cartons on the floor. When I picked them up, he stood up on his back legs and begged so cutely that I fed him all the leftover chunks of beef, though I was getting peckish myself.

I kept hoping I could catch Abby's eye, but she didn't look my way. At half past eleven I knew I was going to have to muscle in or face being stuck here all night. I got up and shook Abby's arm.

'Abby, the last train leaves soon. We need to head off.'

She looked up. 'Oh, right.'

'Why don't you stay here?' Brian rubbed a hand across her shoulders. 'Seems to be what your mate's doing.' He nodded at Claudia, who was still busy with Gabe. I wondered when they'd found the time to breathe.

To my relief Abby shook her head. 'Um, I promised Ros I'd go back with her.'

'Well, she can stay too. She seems pretty attached to that beanbag.'

What an idiot, I thought angrily.

He put his arm round Abby. 'You don't have to go, do you, sweetheart?'

She giggled, not looking at him.

'I've got all my jewellery stuff upstairs. I'll show you how I make earrings. You can keep a pair if you like.'

'That'd be great, but . . . maybe another time? It's just, I said to Ros—'

'Why not now? You don't need your mate to make your decisions. Come on, Abby. You want to stay, you stay – simple as.'

Why wasn't this guy getting it? Realizing I would have to step in, I took her arm.

'No, we really have to go. Now.'

For a moment I thought Brian wasn't going to let go of her. But, after a moment, he did. There was a sulky look on his face, like a kid who hadn't got his own way. Ignoring him, I pulled Abby down the stairs to the front door. The cool air outside felt wonderful after the house's stuffiness.

'That was a pretty long half an hour!' I cried. 'What were you playing at?'

'I was having a good time,' said Abby. 'Brian is so cool, isn't he?'

'So is he your boyfriend now? Or was he too busy slobbering over you to talk?'

'He doesn't slobber! Look, it's obvious he really likes me. He said I have beautiful eyes.'

'Abby, that's the most unoriginal line in the world!'

'How would you know? Has anyone said it to you?'

I looked away.

'Come on, Ros,' Abby said pleadingly. 'Maybe you didn't have the greatest evening, but aren't you happy for me? We both have boyfriends now – isn't that awesome?'

'Oh, shut up, Abby!' I snapped, feeling grumpy, worried and mean all at once. 'Let's just get back, OK?'

out now, I texted to Jonathan. **heres hopin dad isnt bak yet**.

Crossing fingers. Will be online when you get back if you wanna chat.

There were rowdy people in our carriage on the journey home, and though they didn't bother us, I was glad I wasn't alone. Abby chattered away – now that she was out of the house, her don't-care attitude had changed to a second-thoughts attitude. 'It'll be OK,' she kept saying. 'Your dad will be out for ages yet. We'll get away with it.'

But Dad's car was in the drive.

'Oh crap,' Abby whispered.

My mobile showed several missed calls. 'He must've tried

to ring while we were underground,' I said, blowing my breath out slowly and trying to stay calm. 'He's going to hit the roof.'

'Maybe we could sneak in and make out we were in your room all the time . . .'

'You think he won't have looked there?'

'I could still go home,' said Abby in a small voice. 'If I get in without waking my parents, I could pretend we argued or something and I came back. I'll get into trouble, but it won't be as bad.'

This was so unfair! I was the one who'd been sensible, who'd hated every minute of being in that house, and yet I was the one who was going to take the rap.

'Run away then,' I snapped. 'Thanks for nothing.'

'What else can I do? It's bad luck your dad being here so early. I'm sorry, Ros!'

'Look, just go, will you? There's nothing you can do.'

Abby left, looking near to tears. I stared at the front door a long time before opening it. As quietly as I could, I made for the stairs.

'What time do you call this?' Dad appeared in the sitting-room doorway, arms folded and expression cold. 'Do you have any idea how worried I've been? You were supposed to be home almost two hours ago, Ros! Where the hell were you?'

'The cinema.'

'For seven hours?' He gave me a look that made me feel very small indeed. 'Haven't you lied to me enough?'

'I was with Abby the whole time,' I hedged, trying desperately to think of a convincing story. 'It's not like we were in any danger.'

'I don't care if you were with a whole group of people. You're fourteen, and there's no way you should be out this late. Have you been wandering the streets?'

'We only went to Kensington.'

'Kensington! Why Kensington?'

I shrugged.

'You weren't meeting that boy from the Internet, were you?'

'No.' But I'm meeting him tomorrow, I thought, and felt my stomach dive. 'He doesn't even live in London, Dad.'

'Are you lying to me, Rosalind?'

'No, we were just looking around, really. I thought you'd still be out.'

Dad went very red. Massive blunder alert, Ros!

'So you thought you'd go behind my back. Do you do this every time I'm not home?'

'No – this is the first time, honestly. I'm sorry you were worried, but I'm *fine*. Can't we just leave it and go to bed?'

'You're not getting out of this that easily, young lady.

You've let me down tonight; that's selfish, Ros!' He paused, but I had nothing to say. 'Have you ever given a thought to how difficult things have been for me without your mother? Holding down a job and bringing up two girls? There are times I've been as miserable as hell, but I've kept going and tried to be the best dad I can. I thought you understood that I wanted you back by eleven because I care about your safety, not because I'm a mean old man who wants to spoil things.'

I swallowed. How did he know exactly what to say to make me feel most guilty? 'Sorry.'

'You've always been the one with your head screwed on. I don't expect this from you. How am I going to know you're keeping safe when Petra and I go away to Paris at half-term? I only booked that holiday because I thought you girls could look after yourselves for a couple of days. There's no way I'm going if I can't trust you.'

'Sorry,' I mumbled again.

'Go to bed.' He turned from the door, and I saw him go to the drinks cabinet. I hovered, wishing we could get the bad feeling out of the air. He glanced at me as he took out a bottle of whisky.

'I've nothing more to say to you.'

And there was nothing more for me to say. I went upstairs and cried into my pillow, wishing life wasn't so unfair.

★

When I felt a bit better I switched on my computer. Jonathan was online, just like he'd said he'd be. *im in the doghouse*, I told him, trying to type quietly so Dad wouldn't hear. *dad was home*.

Oh crap. Let me guess, he was mad at you.

yup. feel really bad now.

Did you explain?

no way! hed prolly explode if i told him wed been round at an older guys house! so angry – abby said 30 mins & we stayed 2 hrs! just cos she didnt want 2 look stupid in front of every1. >:-(

Maybe she was banking on you making a fuss about going home.

wot do u mean?

No one wants to be the one to break up a party. Sometimes when I was out with Freya and she seemed to be having a good time I'd find out later that she'd wanted to go home but waited for someone else to suggest it. Kind of confusing.

u can say that again. tnx 4 bein on call 4 me.

No worries. It's not like I've anything better to do. Actually, I've had a shit evening myself. Tell you about it when we see each other tomorrow. ☺

Never had a smiley emoticon made me feel less like smiling.

Jonathan
Saturday 27 September, 10.15 a.m.

Mum tried to return to last night's conversation over breakfast, but I avoided getting drawn in. I felt very relieved when she dropped me off at the station and I was alone – or rather, alone until I saw Lucy standing by the barriers a few feet away.

Just my luck! I tried to hide behind the vending machine, but she spotted me and bounced over.

'Hi, Jonathan! What are you doing here?'

'Waiting for a train?' I suggested, but my sarcasm was lost on her.

She waved her carrier bag in my face. 'Look, new computer games! I'm heading to my friend's in Ipswich to try them out. You up for joining us?'

'Um, thanks but no thanks. I'm off to London to meet a mate and then stay at my girlfriend's.'

It had only occurred to me after agreeing to meet Ros that Freya wouldn't necessarily like the thought of me having lunch with another girl. After some thought, I decided not to tell her. Freya and I were going through a rocky enough time as it was. What she didn't know couldn't hurt her.

Lucy sat next to me on the train. After babbling about the games for a while she said, 'We should hang out more. Want to go to the cinema sometime?'

I blinked. 'As in . . . a date?'

'I guess. How about it?'

'Come on, Lucy. You know I'm with Freya. I'd never cheat on her.'

'You know what pisses me off?' Lucy burst out. 'Since she came along and you did that concert, you think you're in another league. We used to get on; now you just grunt whenever I try to chat to you.'

She was right, I guessed. We had hung out at school every so often, and a couple of times we'd met up in the evening. It all seemed a long time ago now. 'That's because I'm always half asleep on that zombie bus.'

'No, it's because I'm not "cool enough" to be seen with, because Freya gave you this whole new image and you're still clinging on to it even now she isn't around –'

'Hey! That's well out of order!'

'But you're lying to yourself! You've dropped all your other interests – you could have joined college gaming club with me and made lots of mates but you won't because you're scared you'll look sad, or people will pick on you or something.'

'People did pick on me, remember?'

'At school! We've moved on since then – not that you seem to have noticed!'

'Lucy –' I said, drawing breath. But she was on her feet and heading down the carriage, even though we wouldn't get into Ipswich for a good ten minutes. What the heck had all that been about? I mulled over it for a few minutes before deciding Lucy didn't understand. Maybe I was more image-conscious these days, but without Freya and music, hanging on to who I'd become was about the only thing I had. Why did girls get crushes on guys with steady girlfriends anyway? Seemed pretty stupid to obsess over someone you couldn't have.

My train arrived at Liverpool Street on time. I went to the meeting place, the AMT coffee stand. Ros wasn't there yet, so I waited, feeling eager yet oddly nervous too.

Rosalind
10.25 a.m.

My retro hat was gone. I discovered this when, too anxious to do anything else, I started getting ready early. Must have left it at the aren't-artists', I realized. That was just wonderful – another problem to sort out.

I stuck my head round the door of Olivia's room. She was sitting in bed listening to the Killers and texting her boyfriend.

'Livy, can I borrow a tenner?'

'Why don't you ask Dad?'

Dad hadn't said a word to me at breakfast. He was out at neighbourhood watch this morning, which was just as well, as I had a feeling he'd stop me going out again. It was also lucky he hadn't got close last night. I'd realized this morning that my hair smelt of weed and cigarette smoke and washed it thoroughly.

'Dad's out,' I said. 'Please.'

She sighed. 'There's some cash in the pocket of my jacket.'

'Thanks. You wouldn't be extra nice and let me borrow clothes too, would you?'

Olivia raised her eyebrows. 'You know they won't fit you.'

'You don't need to remind me.'

She watched as I looked through her stuff, feeling like a sticky-fingered toddler. I took out a denim skirt and a stripy strapped top. If I put them with a necklace and my school tights, I might look OK. I returned to my room, locking the door. The skirt proved to be unwearable without a belt and the top sagged when I bent over, but they were still better than anything in my wardrobe.

When I went out to pick up my tights from the laundry basket I bumped into Olivia on the landing.

'You're not going out like that, are you?' she demanded.

'What?' I said defensively.

She grabbed my wrist. 'God, don't you know anything? Come here.'

Olivia pulled me into her room. She opened one of her drawers and dangled a bra in front of me.

'Put this on.'

'It won't fit.'

'I know, just put it on.'

I turned to the wall and did as she said. When I turned back Olivia was armed with a box of tissues.

'Pad it with these. It'll give you a bit of shape.'

I did as she said. Then I went to the mirror.

'Wow,' I said, tilting to view myself from one angle, then another. 'I actually look female.'

'You'll look better if you put on a bit of make-up. Here, let me do it.'

She sat me down on her bed and got out an eyeliner. She smudged it round my eyes then applied mascara, threatening to stop if I dared blink.

'I don't look much like me any more; I guess that's a good thing,' I said, admiring the results. 'Thanks, Livy.'

'No problem. Where are you off to, anyway?'

I smiled and didn't answer.

Feeling a little more confident, I messed around with shoes and hairclips until it was time to go. Knowing Dad would ask questions too if he saw me like this, I left quickly.

I was halfway to the station when the doubts I'd been

trying to ignore caught up with me. Everyone had said over and over again what a bad idea it was to meet strangers from the Internet – and now the time had come, I wasn't brave enough to ignore them. What if everyone else was right about Jonathan, and I was wrong? I hesitated for a long moment, then turned and made my way to Abby's house.

Abby's mum gave a double take when she answered the door – probably wondering where I suddenly got boobs from. It was clear from the way she was acting that Abby had got away with it last night.

Abby looked surprised to see me when her mum showed me into her room.

'Ros! I thought . . . Wow! Who made you over? You look older – really cool. I love it!'

I wasn't in the mood for this. Instead I brought up the night before – and it was just as Jonathan had said. Abby hadn't wanted to be the one to break up the party.

'Didn't want to look bad in front of Claudia and the guys,' she mumbled.

'Oh, right!' I snapped. 'So you'd have moaned and groaned about how you so desperately wanted to stay, but had to go with boring old Ros, and I'd have been the party pooper. That's mean, Abby.'

'They're not your friends. You've said you don't care what they think.'

I do and I don't, and nothing makes sense at the moment, I thought. 'Whatever! Abby, I need you to come with me to Liverpool Street. I said I'd meet Jonathan there and I could really do with company, just in case – well, just in case he's not who he said. And there's another problem.' I drew a long breath. 'He thinks I'm Olivia.'

Shamefacedly, I explained.

Abby looked at me with big eyes. 'Oh, Ros! Why do you apologize for yourself all the time? If Jonathan's as great as you say, he'll like you for you.'

'I don't know about that.'

'Funny kind of boyfriend,' Abby muttered, picking up her bag. 'Don't start crying, Ros. You'll mess up your make-up. Like I said, it looks really nice. Is that tissue in your bra?'

'I never used to tell lies like this,' I sniffled. 'If love's meant to tell you who you are, then I don't want to be me.'

'Don't say that. There are loads of good things about you.'

I wiped my nose on my sleeve. 'Like what?'

Abby gave me a hug. 'Like you're my best friend.'

On the tube, I willed the journey to last forever. What was I going to say to Jonathan? He'd know I'd lied the moment he saw me and 'I wanted you to think I was pretty' sounded such a desperate excuse.

'Best just to tell the truth,' Abby kept saying. 'It's not

nice but I don't see how you can get out of this one.'

We'd texted a friend from school before setting off. I thought it might be good if a third person knew what I was doing – just in case.

I nearly bottled out when we got off the train. With each step, I felt sicker. Not 'uppity' any more, I thought, and took a deep breath as the escalator carried us to ground level.

I led Abby to the coffee stand the long way, bobbing behind people and hoping Jonathan's train had been delayed. No such luck.

'God!' Abby whispered, catching sight of him. 'So he isn't a weird old man after all. He's really fit.'

There could be no mistake – he even had a guitar case on his shoulder. He was leaning against a billboard with his hands in his pockets and I guessed he'd been waiting a while.

I forgot my nerves for a moment. He'd been telling the truth! I was so relieved that I wanted to sing it out. Everything we'd shared had been real – *Jonathan* was real, and he was even better-looking than he had been in the photo.

'What're you going to do?' Abby's voice brought me back to reality. I ducked behind a timetable board next to the coffee stand, peeping out to keep an eye on Jonathan. My heart was pounding so forcefully that I was worried it might pop out of my chest. The things I'd wondered – what it would feel like to touch his hair, to share a kiss – crowded my mind and the last of my confidence crumbled. Forget about pretending I was nearly seventeen and pretty, there was also the nightmare of Abby thinking he was my boyfriend. How had there come to be so many lies?

'Excuse me,' It was a voice with a funny country accent that spoke, and in a heartbeat I realized it was Jonathan, addressing a man waiting for coffee. 'Do you have the time?'

The man pointed to the station clock, which was in plain sight.

Jonathan laughed, colouring slightly. 'Oops. I need new specs.'

Hi, Jonathan, I'm Rosalind, and I'm sorry I'm a total coward, but I wanted to impress you.

Jonathan was pacing now. Asking the people at the coffee stand if there'd been delays on the tube. Beginning to look annoyed.

'Ros,' Abby whispered again, 'what are you going to do?'

Hi, Jonathan, I'm Rosalind, and I think you look great.

He took his phone out. I felt my pocket buzz. I didn't pick up.

Hi, Jonathan, I'm Rosalind, and I might be in love with you.

'Ros! Come on.' Abby tugged my arm, pulling me out from behind the board and towards Jonathan.

'Abby! Let go!' But it was too late. Jonathan glanced at us – and for a long moment our eyes met. I froze. Oh God, this was it! Beside me, Abby giggled nervously. Jonathan gave her a funny look and placed his mobile to his ear. After a few seconds, I realized. He didn't recognize me! He thought we were just two silly little girls! Relief and bitter disappointment mingled inside me as I watched him turn his back on us.

'Hey, Freya,' he said into his phone. 'Just a quick call. Can you remind me of the number of your aunt's house again? . . . Fifty-seven, Ridgemont Street? OK. And that's Richmond station . . . See you soon. I'll be earlier than I thought.' Jonathan stuffed his mobile back in his pocket and nodded to the coffee-stand people. 'Thanks for your help. I'll be off now.'

'Thought you were waiting for someone,' said the woman at the till.

'I thought I was too,' said Jonathan. 'Seems she's not so keen.'

'Ros!' Abby hissed. I wanted to scream out that I was keen, keener than he could possibly know, but I couldn't find the words, let alone walk up to him.

'If you see a pretty girl with long brown hair come and wait here, could you tell her to give Jonathan a ring? Thanks.' Jonathan gave the station a last sweeping glance and moved off. As he disappeared into the crowd I saw him raise his phone to his ear again. A moment later my mobile went off. It seemed to vibrate for a very long time. When it stopped I took it out and saw that he'd left voicemail.

'Ros, this is Jonathan. I waited twenty minutes and you didn't come, so I guess you don't want to meet me after all. I'm not sticking about so I've gone to Freya's. If you still want to see me, give me a ring. Bye.'

'Ros, run.' Abby's voice seemed to come from very far away. 'You can still catch up with him.'

'No, I can't,' I said, and started to cry, tears running through my eyeliner in inky streaks. I felt in my pocket for a tissue, then, as it didn't matter any more, took one from my bra cup and blew my nose on that instead.

What if he didn't want to speak to me after this?

5. Out to Lunch

Jonathan
12.55 p.m.

I couldn't believe it. Ros didn't seem the kind of person who'd stand me up. She was always online when she said she'd be, and by her own admission annoyingly sensible. I wanted to make excuses for her, but unless I got a message soon, I'd just have to face it: she didn't want to see me.

All those evenings we'd typed till our fingers were sore surely meant something to her. Funny how this girl I'd never met was suddenly so important to me. For a moment I wondered if Ros really was who she said she was, but I couldn't bring myself to seriously consider that.

At least I still had something to look forward to – seeing Freya. I cheered up a little. This weekend was bound to be better than the last one – it couldn't be any worse. Maybe then it wouldn't matter so much that Ros hadn't shown.

Auntie Phil's house was a semi down a quiet road near the river. A slim woman with fashionable glasses and very carefully arranged hair answered the door.

'Are you Jonathan? Freya's out.'

'I did call and tell her I was going to be early.' I smiled, hoping to break the ice. 'Any idea where she's gone?'

'One of the coffee shops down the high street, I expect; she said she was meeting a friend. Can't tell you which, and my taxi's due in a minute. You'll have to leave your things here and go and find her.'

I decided not to ask if I could wait in the house. Her tone implied that it wasn't up for discussion. I dumped my bag in the hall.

'By high street, you mean the area around the station, right?'

Auntie Phil nodded. I headed off. Freya didn't pick up when I called her mobile, so I left a message. She'd ring soon – Freya was always fiddling with her phone. And there could only be so many coffee shops to look in.

A Starbucks, a Coffee Republic and two Costas later I still hadn't found her. It seemed like I'd walked past a billion shops and I was wary of going too far. Freya still wasn't picking up, and it would be useless asking people if they'd seen her. Maybe she'd got distracted by clothes shops? I peered through several windows without any luck. By now an hour and a half had passed. I mooched along the street, feeling pissed off. First Ros, now Freya. And to add to the general crapness of what should have been a fun day, it started to rain.

At about half five my phone rang.

'Jonathan, where are you?' asked Freya.

'Inside Coffee Republic having a very late lunch,' I said. 'Where the hell are you? I've been wandering round for hours!'

'Don't be like that. I was with my friend Emma and something came up.'

'Then why didn't you call me? You knew I was going to be early.'

'Jonny, I'm sorry; I'll make it up to you, I promise. Me and Emma will be at the conservatoire in an hour – meet outside Embankment station? There's a concert there tonight – student showcase, right up your street – that sound like a plan?'

Very clever, bringing your friend so I can't let you know how pissed off I am, I thought. I headed to Embankment and hung about by the entrance, feeling more and more annoyed as the minutes passed. When – half an hour later – I caught sight of the top of Freya's head in the crowd, I was all set to demand an explanation. But as she got closer, my anger died. She was pushing a wheelchair.

I wasn't sure what to say as we stood in the queue outside the conservatoire. Though I didn't mean to, I kept glancing at Emma. She was quite pretty, I guessed. Her hair was so fair it was almost white; paired with the pale blue coat she was wearing, it made her look a bit ghostlike. Freya had mentioned Emma a few times, but she'd never said she was disabled.

Freya apologized for leaving me waiting. 'I thought Auntie Phil would let you in so you could go on the computer or something,' she said. 'If this happens again, there's a spare key hidden in the bush by the door – go ahead and use it.'

Somehow I couldn't find it in me to be angry any more. Besides, the conservatoire was amazing, all quirky and olde England, right by the Thames. I admired the view, watching headlights from buses and cabs weave their way through offices and apartments. My village only had a few street lights and the shop closed at six, so most people stayed in after dark. I could get used to London, I reckoned.

In the foyer, Freya went to get drinks, leaving me with Emma. I racked my mind for something to say and came out with, 'You a student here too?'

Emma nodded. 'Violin. Freya told me you play guitar.'

'That's right. Have done since I was tiny.' Then, because I couldn't help it: 'She talks about me then?'

'Sometimes. You're a very lucky guy, you know.'

'To have Freya? Yeah, I know.'

'As in . . . *really* lucky.'

I wasn't sure what she was getting at. 'What d'you mean?'

Emma glanced across the foyer at a group of people our age. Though a couple had waved at her, it was clear they weren't going to come over.

'I've learned a lot about people in the last few weeks,' she said. 'When I started here, everyone was nice, but they kept their distance. Freya was the only one who bothered to get to know me. She really goes the extra mile to make sure I get included and have a good time. Can't tell you what a difference that makes.'

Freya reappeared with three glasses of orange juice.

'What're you blushing for?' she asked, handing round the drinks.

I shrugged, not wanting to say that though Emma's words had made me feel really proud of Freya, they'd also made me feel I didn't know very much about her new life at all.

Luckily Freya didn't wait for an answer. She took the wheelchair with her spare hand. 'Come on, let's join the gang.'

Soon we were chatting with the other students and I started to feel more comfortable. People seemed interested in me – they seemed to find my stories of country life funny. And for once, it wasn't because of Freya. Most of them didn't even know she had a boyfriend, which surprised me a little. But it was good to know I fitted in – after being ignored so much at college, I'd started to wonder if there was something wrong with me.

The concert was a student showcase, which reminded me of the act I'd done with Freya. The standard was high, but that was no surprise. These kids had the best tuition in the country – like I could have had. And, even though I was enjoying the music, I started to feel angry at Mum and Dad all over again.

But maybe I wasn't as talented as I wanted to believe. I hadn't composed anything all term – I needed Freya to bounce ideas off and spot notes that didn't work – and I hadn't even felt like playing recently. And these guys were so good. With such competition, could I have even got into the conservatoire? I didn't know – but now I'd had a taste, I wanted it. Badly.

I glanced at Freya. She was watching the performance with a smile on her face, and suddenly I felt like shaking her. I wanted to shout that I hated the choices my parents had made and being stuck in a place with people who didn't understand me, and that if I could turn back the clock I would in an instant, and that I just hoped she appreciated how damn lucky she was.

After the show finished, we saw Emma home. The buses were supposedly wheelchair-friendly, but it was a hassle getting on and off and I couldn't help admiring Freya's patience. Near the end of the journey a gang of kids got on and started making loud comments about 'spazzes'. Without even glancing their way, Freya stuck her finger up at them.

'You never mentioned she was in a wheelchair,' I said as

we walked to the underground station after saying goodbye to Emma.

'She's isn't all the time – only when she gets tired.' Freya looked at me, smiling. 'Why, did it surprise you?'

I shrugged. A lot of teenagers would think twice about being seen with someone in a wheelchair, but Freya genuinely didn't mind. That was really kind – but then Freya always had been – which made how she'd been with me recently all the more worrying.

'Anyway,' Freya said, 'enough about Emma. Did you like the conservatoire?'

'Yeah. Course.'

'You don't sound very happy.'

'I'm fine.' I thought it was better not to mention that I was still seething with jealousy. 'Just . . . guess today made me think. It feels like everything I care about's slipping away from me.'

'You mean me?'

For a moment I felt panicked. It was one thing for me to worry, but another to hear her acknowledge there were problems. 'Freya, I love you, you know that. But it's been weird since you came here.'

Freya looked serious. 'You surely didn't expect everything to stay the same?'

Maybe I'm naive, but I had. Back at the start of summer, when everything had been going so well, it hadn't occurred to me that distance might strain our relationship. Now though – it wasn't just paranoia telling me things weren't working.

I took her hand. 'I don't want to lose you. Sure, we talk, but you can't kiss or hold someone over a phone, and though I know that's not what a relationship's about, it's reassuring. Sometimes I'm not sure you care any more.'

'What makes you think that?'

It was hard to answer without launching into self-pity.

'Maybe we need to talk more,' I said. 'Truth is, there's a lot on my mind at the moment.' And I found myself telling her about college, my parents and music. When I was done, Freya ran a hand through her hair, shaking her head. We were on a train now, standing by the doors because all the seats were taken.

'This isn't what you want to hear . . . but really, your life isn't that bad.'

'Easy for you to say.' I didn't mean to snap, but I felt defensive and vulnerable.

Freya looked at me with a funny expression. 'Grow up, Jonny.'

'What? Freya, this is real to me!'

'You say you hate college; well, I say, college is what you make of it. Sure, you don't want to be there, but are you going to angst about that for two years or try to make the best of it? Totally understand you being upset about the music, but honestly, you don't need to go to music school or even have an A level to go professional. How about you advertise for music buddies in the area, form a band?'

'I could, I s'pose, but—'

'Why not? Jonny, you get grade As on automatic – how do you think it feels to be me, who wasn't born smart like you and has to slog for halfway decent grades? How do you think it feels to be Emma? She has multiple sclerosis. Some days she's fine, but others she throws up, sees strange stuff, and sometimes when she has a bad attack she ends up in hospital on a drip. Today wasn't good and we had to get out the wheelchair; that's why I couldn't meet up with you.' She paused. 'I wish you'd take life on the chin a bit more! I know it sounds harsh, but the only person who's stopping you being happy is you.'

Suddenly I really wished I could talk to Ros. She sometimes told me things I didn't want to hear, but she always managed it in a way that made me feel optimistic rather than small and mean.

'Well,' I said off-handedly, 'least I know what you think now.'

Freya laid her hand on my chest. 'Don't get all huffy. We can still have a nice weekend.'

I sighed. 'Yeah.'

There was no point in saying the other thing on my mind – that this London Freya felt even less like the Freya

I'd said goodbye to than I realized. Had she simply moved on, or had I been deluding myself?

Rosalind
Saturday 4 October, 4.00 p.m.

All week I couldn't bear to talk to Jonathan. Several emails from him had appeared in my inbox.

From: 'Jonathan H. Oxley'
To: 'Ros Fielding'
Sunday 28 September, 10:06

Ros?
You must have got the messages I left on your phone by now. Sorry if I was pushy but I assumed you'd want to meet me. Did something happen or did you never intend to come? I thought we were friends.
Come on. Talk to me, Ros.

That was the worst one. He sounded so hurt. Several times I nearly replied, but I couldn't think of what to say.

After talking almost every day, it felt like there was a huge gap in my life. Not knowing what Jono was doing or if he was OK was driving me mad, and I kept thinking of things I wanted to tell him, stuff no one else would understand. I read over some old emails, hoping they might make me feel as though he was there, but they only made things worse.

Most of all, I hated knowing he'd spent the weekend with Freya. It was wrong to resent someone I'd never met, but I did. However hard I tried, however much I cared about Jonathan, it would never be enough, because she was – and always would be – his number one. I wondered for the hundredth time what he saw in her. Sure, she was stunning, and the music was a common interest, but I didn't believe they could be on the same wavelength – not like we were. Maybe one day Jono would realize that.

Ten o'clock on Saturday found me at High Street Kensington. I was wearing a pair of seventies flared dungarees which I'd picked up in another charity shop. It took me a while to find Gabe's house. The streets seemed different in the light of day. The doorbell was broken, so I rapped on the door. After a while it was thrown open.

'You! What the hell time is this for a social call?'

It was Hugh, hunched like a primeval man who'd slept in a hedge. Feeling myself blush, I looked away. I'd seen shirtless guys on TV, but for some reason Hugh made me feel uncomfortable.

'I left my hat here,' I said. 'I hope you haven't thrown it away.'

'Hah! Cute way-too-suspicious Ros. Nice flares, by the way.' He sloped up the stairs scratching his shoulder. I closed the door and followed him to the sitting room, where I was almost bowled over by a very excited Dog. He ran round me in circles, then rolled over on his back. Touched that he remembered me, I knelt down and scratched his tummy.

'He likes you.'

I looked up at Hugh. 'Well, I like him.'

Giving Dog a final pat, I got up and looked round the room, which was in a state.

'Nothing to do with me, if that's what you're wondering,' Hugh said. 'Some of Graham's rubbish mates got pissed and thought smashing the place up would be exquisite entertainment.'

'So that's why the doorbell isn't working.'

'They did worse than break the doorbell, they broke the telly! Bastards.'

'You'll live.' I found my hat, underneath the beanbag I'd been sitting on.

'You woke me up, y'know,' said Hugh. 'I hope you're happy.'

'Sorry. You can go back to bed now.'

He yawned and pulled on a shirt that was lying across one of the couches. 'Maybe I'll stretch my legs instead.

Where are you off to, cute Ros?'

'Somewhere.' I made for the stairs and out on to the street. Hugh ambled after me. Dog slipped out too and trotted off down the street, sniffing at rubbish bins.

'Is it safe for him to wander about?' I asked. 'He might get run over.'

'Not that one; he's a survivor. 'Sides, not many cars come down here.' Hugh tilted his face skywards. 'So this is what morning feels like.'

I made a non-committal noise and we walked in silence to the station. 'Bye,' I said, as I fed my travel card into the ticket barrier. My train was waiting on the platform and I hopped on, thankful to have lost Hugh. But as I sat down I saw him sauntering down the carriage.

'We going shopping?' he asked, taking the next seat. I glared at him.

'Stop following me.'

'I'm not following you. I'm accompanying you.'

'You're wasting your money.'

'Nope.' He waved an Oyster card at me. 'This is Graham's. I borrow it every so often. My good luck it was in my pocket from yesterday, isn't it?'

I stared at him. He gave me a big grin.

'Off to see your boyfriend, sweetheart?'

'Do you specialize in annoying people?'

'You shouldn't be so secretive. Makes me curious.'

'Don't you have anything better to do – like finding a job? You keep saying how skint you are.'

'Easier said than done. You seen the unemployment figures? I'd rather live off Graham for a couple of months than fill out loads of job apps that get chucked straight in the bin.'

The train pulled into Earl's Court. I got off and waited for the Richmond train. When Hugh stepped on to the new train and sat beside me I began to feel a little panicked. If he was doing this as a joke, it really wasn't funny any more. Trying to sound firm, I said, 'I'm not going anywhere interesting. Why do you care, anyway?'

'I'm bored, and you're a funny kid I haven't figured out yet.'

The train arrived at West Kensington. Several people got on and took the remaining seats, leaving an elderly lady on her feet. Hugh stood up.

'Want to sit down?'

The old lady took his seat, thanking Hugh and telling him he was a gentleman. Hugh smiled and moved to hold on to one of the poles by the doors. Suddenly I was confused. The last time I had seen anyone give up their seat had been ages ago. It was easier to pretend you hadn't seen, like everyone else on the carriage had just now.

When we neared Richmond, I stood up.

Hugh raised his eyebrows. 'Why're you looking at me like that?'

'You gave up your seat.'

'So?'

'Nothing,' I said quickly. Hugh rolled his eyes.

We got off. After gaining my bearings, I found my way off the high street, across the green and to a residential street near the river. In the middle of the road was an island with a few trees, and I sat down with my back against one.

'I'm hungry,' Hugh said. 'Want a bite to eat? There was a Tesco Metro back there.'

Somehow, it didn't feel OK any more to tell him to leave me alone. Hugh headed off and returned with a bag of doughnuts. He sat down beside me. I took one when he offered.

'You and your doughnuts,' I said.

'Doughnuts make a very respectable meal. Out to lunch, that's what we are.'

'It isn't lunchtime yet.'

'Breakfast, brunch, whatever. So why are we here?'

After just a moment's hesitation I took out the ring binder I'd been carrying under my arm and showed Hugh Freya's photograph. 'Fine. I'm waiting for her, OK? Don't say anything when she comes out. I don't want her to know who I am.'

'Pretty girl.' Before I could stop him, he had flicked to the next plastic wallet, which contained a picture of a catwalk model I'd cut from one of Olivia's magazines.

'Give that back.' I tried to grab it, but he moved to one side and turned the page, this time to a newspaper clipping of a glamorous actress. I reached across and managed to snatch it away. Not looking at him, I crossed my arms over the folder and hugged it to my chest.

'You weird kid,' said Hugh, sounding amused. 'Collect photos of hot girls, do we?'

'I like looking at pretty people in pretty clothes.' It wasn't a crime, but I couldn't help but sound defensive. 'Lots of girls keep pictures of fashion models if they like their clothes. Anyway, I use them for drawing reference.'

'The first girl's not from a magazine.'

'I'm curious about her – that's all.'

Hugh gave me a look, but didn't say anything. I wished he'd go away. Even though he possibly wasn't as bad as I'd thought, I felt embarrassed. Minutes passed. A few people came by, some giving us curious glances. We probably looked a strange pair. At about one, the door to number fifty-seven opened and Freya stepped out. Just like with Jonathan at the station, it felt odd coming face to face with someone I'd seen in photographs. I'd secretly been hoping Freya was one of those people who only looked great through a camera lens, but she was just as vibrant-looking in the flesh – the kind of girl people didn't forget. Today she was wearing a floral-print minidress and bright green tights. I did my best to look nonchalant as she walked past.

Hugh, however, wolf-whistled. Freya paused and turned her head. He gave her a broad smile and a wave. She regarded us quizzically for a moment, then moved on.

'I told you not to say anything!' I hissed.

'I didn't. Since when was whistling talking?'

'Go home!'

'No way. I'm far too interested.'

I got up and walked after Freya, who was almost out of sight. She headed to the station. I waited until a couple of people had got between us and followed her through the barriers and on to a train. I was ready to duck down if she looked my way, but she got out a magazine and read it until we changed on to the Central Line.

'We're going shopping after all,' remarked Hugh as we got out at Notting Hill Gate.

Freya disappeared into a shop called Retro Babe.

'Going in?' asked Hugh.

'No. She'll notice us. I just want to see what she buys.'

'Why are you stalking her?'

I backed away from the window, almost colliding with a passer-by. 'I'm not.'

'What? You waited outside her home and followed her here. In my book, that's stalking. This a random hobby of yours, or is Miss Sixties special?'

'I'm just checking her out,' I mumbled. 'Not against the law, is it?'

'Ah! Hadn't got you down as that way inclined, but if it's what floats your boat—'

'Shut up, Hugh, she's not the one I'm really interested in, OK? If all you're going to do is poke fun, you can just get stuffed!'

Hugh looked at me a moment, then nodded. 'I get it. She's your boyfriend's girlfriend.'

I couldn't disguise my surprise. 'How did you work that out?'

'You're dressing like her. Biggest telltale there is. Listen, kid, however much you want to, you can't become her. You should get out before you do anything you'll regret. Cos stalking, you know, is gonna turn you into a crazy psycho sooner or later.'

I stared at him, biting my lip.

Freya reappeared clutching a carrier bag. Seeing a bus just down the road, she ran towards it, waving her arm, her kitten heels clicking along the pavement. On automatic I followed, flashing my travel card to the driver, and took the seat behind her. Hugh sat across the aisle. I turned my face to the window so I didn't have to look at him.

'He's not worth it, sweetheart,' Hugh said softly. Then, sharply, 'Hey, Miss Sixties, the kid here's been stalking you.'

Freya turned from inspecting the shoes she'd bought, looking startled. Her eyes connected with mine before I bolted from my seat, pressing one of the stop buttons. The bus came to a halt and I jumped off, not looking back. Noticing a litter bin, I jammed my ring binder inside. Then I walked, and kept on walking. I didn't care where I ended up. I just wanted to get away.

How could I have become so wound up in Jonathan that I hadn't realized following his girlfriend was creepy? Stalking wasn't normal, not in any way. And why did being friends with Jonathan seem so important? I'd never even met him. It made no sense to feel so strongly, but I did.

I really ought to leave it, like Hugh had said.

But I knew I wasn't going to.

6. On the Phone

From: 'Jonathan H. Oxley'
To: 'Ros Fielding'
Date: Sunday 12 October, 10:30

Hello

Even if you're not going to speak to me again, at least let me know you're OK. Still can't figure what I did to scare you off – I thought we were friends. So, LAST EMAIL. If you don't reply I'm not going to spam your mailbox any more. Think I've got the message.

J.

From: 'Ros Fielding'
To: 'Jonathan H. Oxley'
Date: Monday 13 October, 21:05

jonathan

i am very sorry 4 not showin up. there was a last min family thing i had to go 2.

i hav not been online this wk cos i was worried u wd b mad at me. r u?

i wd still like 2 talk 2 u if u want 2 talk 2 me. i miss u.

ros x

From: 'Jonathan H. Oxley'
To: 'Ros Fielding'
Date: Monday 13 October, 23:57

Hi, Rosalind

I'm not mad, just pissed off. You could have let me know you weren't going to show – I felt a right idiot hanging about, and I had a weird weekend at Freya's afterwards.

Jono

From: 'Ros Fielding'
To: 'Jonathan H. Oxley'
Date: Tuesday 14 October, 07:37

jono,

i am sorry i did not call or email u. i guess i was just bein stupid & thinkin u wouldnt want 2 b friends any more.

luv ros x

From: 'Jonathan H. Oxley'
To: 'Ros Fielding'
Date: Tuesday 14 October, 14:15

Hi Ros

Tell you what, let's just put this behind us. Promise I'm not angry. ☺ Smiley face, see?

Jono

Jonathan
Saturday 18 October, 4.40 p.m.

'Family thing'. I wasn't convinced, but I decided to let it go. I'd missed Ros, more than I thought I could miss someone

I'd never met. Funny how talking on a screen seemed more real than the conversations I had with people at college. I could never tell *them* how worried I was about Freya. After the evening at the conservatoire, the weekend had gone OK, but I'd felt a distance between us that hadn't been there previously. Even my birthday present to her – genuine sixties gloves I'd found online – hadn't helped. And despite me saying we needed to talk more, if anything we talked less. Since I'd come home, Freya was increasingly difficult to get hold of, not always returning my calls and rarely chatting long when she did. She said mid-term performances were taking up all her time. Perhaps I was being paranoid again, but I did wonder how true that was.

maybe shes just busy with other ppl, Rosalind said one night. *she still likes u, but ur just not no1 rite now*.

I felt special before. Now I get the feeling I've become a bore.

wd u b sayin this if that wkend b4 her bday had gone ok?

Probably not.

then things r ok. itll b bak 2 normal when shes home @ xmas.

Ros could be right – I knew I read too much into Freya's behaviour. It had been so easy to know what she was thinking when I saw her every day. She'd never been shy about showing how much she liked me either. One time at school, when I'd been waiting for her to show up at lunch, a couple of guys who fancied her had started to take the piss out of me. When Freya arrived she didn't waste time with words; she grabbed my face and snogged me until the guys slunk away. 'Best thing I could think of to shut them up,' she'd explained. That was one of my favourite memories of Freya, but today it made me feel horribly sad. Before we'd started going out, I'd been a much simpler person. While I didn't want to go back, life had been a lot easier when I only thought about how I could modify the inside of the computer to make it faster and more powerful, or which DVDs and video games I should spend my monthly allowance on. Sometimes I felt I was two people who hadn't even met.

College was still crap. The novelty of being in a new place had worn off and, like many students, I was bored. The Student Union tried to cheer us up by organizing a disco and placing tickets and a free-drink voucher in everyone's pigeonhole – everyone's except mine, that was. Though I knew the person handing out the tickets had probably just made an error, I couldn't help feeling it had been done deliberately. And what was the point of going to some stupid dance where no one would talk to me?

Sick of everything, I called Freya on Saturday afternoon, hoping for a long conversation.

She didn't pick up.

Like always, I thought angrily. It shouldn't be this way. I should be able to speak to my girlfriend whenever I needed to. In the old days I'd have gone round her house if I couldn't get through on the phone. Mind you – what was stopping me now?

Mum and Dad grumbled when I begged for a lift to the station.

'It would be good to have some notice when you're going to London for the weekend,' Mum said. 'Honestly, Jonathan! Have a thought for us – and your bank balance, for that matter. Train tickets aren't exactly cheap.'

'Sorry. Forgot.' I looked as sheepish as I could. Somehow, I thought it would be better if they didn't know this was a spur-of-the-moment thing.

Thanks to delays and me getting on the wrong underground train, it was nine by the time I got to Richmond. The door to Auntie Phil's house was ajar.

'Freya?' I called.

Emma came out of the sitting room, on her feet and looking a lot brighter than she had at the conservatoire. 'Freya!' she shouted. 'Your boyfriend's here.'

Freya appeared at the top of the stairs, hair in disarray and an eyeliner stick in her hand. 'What – Jonathan?'

I gave her a wave. 'Surprise visit.'

Freya came down the stairs.

I laughed. 'You look like you've seen a ghost.'

'I'm just . . . well, surprised. You're not usually spontaneous.' Her mouth quivered, then she pushed it into a bright smile.

'Is this a bad time?'

'Course not. Why don't you say hello to my friends? My aunt's on holiday, so everyone's come over.'

Freya disappeared into the kitchen before I could ask to talk to her alone. A gang of girls I didn't recognize were mucking about with a wok, all dressed for a night out. There were also a couple of guys. One smacked Freya on the backside as she entered.

'No bunny-girl costume tonight? I'm disappointed.'

Freya giggled. 'Shh. Adam, this is my boyfriend.'

Adam gave me a glance. 'Oh! Hardly one of those muscle-bound film stars you've got pinned on your wall, is he?'

She poked him in the ribs. 'Don't be mean.'

'It's OK,' I said. 'No offence taken.' I looked at Freya. 'Can I talk to you – in private?'

Freya hesitated.

'Just ten minutes. It's really important.'

'Oh, OK.'

I followed her out of the kitchen, up the stairs and into her room. It smelt of perfume; the macho film stars smirked down at me from the walls. As Freya closed the door I caught sight of her mobile, on the desk by her make-up. It was on.

'You knew I was trying to call you,' I said. 'Why didn't you pick up?'

'I was busy.'

'I wanted to speak to you.'

'Told you, I was busy.'

'Couldn't you have sent me a text? I really needed to talk. I said so when I left voicemail.'

'Yeah, well, I don't have any credit.'

'There's a landline!'

'I know, but Auntie Phil doesn't like me using it for long conversations!'

I went to the desk and picked up the phone.

'Give me that,' said Freya, but I had already dialled the service number.

'Your credit is ten pounds and forty-one pence,' I quoted, laying it back down.

'Stop staring at me, Jonny. It's scary.'

'Since you came here, I've been the one putting the effort into making us work,' I said. 'You never reply to my texts or emails now, and there are always excuses for why we can't chat long. It never occurred to me that you were lying.'

'Look, Jonathan . . .'

'You don't care about me any more, do you?'

'Of course I do! You're a friend, but—'

'You don't love me. I love you.'

Freya fingered a lock of her hair. 'Don't say that. Love's a very big word.'

I shook my head. 'Please just be honest.'

She placed her hands on my shoulders. 'Jonny, I'm so sorry . . . but I think it's time we called it a day.'

The last year zipped through my mind. Freya and me at the opticians, choosing my new glasses. Freya and me picking up exam results, celebrating afterwards. Freya and me at the cinema, bowling, a concert, round each other's houses.

'What did I do wrong?' I asked. 'Is there someone else?'

'You're a lovely guy.' She patted my shoulders. 'I want to stay friends. But the truth is, since I came here – I've been feeling that you're . . . well . . . a bit needy – and I don't think I can give you what you want any more.'

My mouth opened – and stayed open. No words would come out.

'I know you wanted to be the perfect boyfriend. Calling all the time, planning these amazing romantic dinners – that was nice, really, and maybe you'll find a girlfriend who'll appreciate all that, but – well, maybe I've changed. London's opened my eyes.'

'Then I'll change too – just tell me what to do.'

'It's not as easy as that. Look at us, Jonny. Without music, do we really have much in common?'

I took her hands and squeezed them. 'Music's a huge thing. It's what we both care about most, right? Little differences shouldn't matter, not if we love each other.'

'Let go. You're hurting.'

I released my hold, and she stepped back, the colour rising in her cheeks.

'You've put so much pressure on me,' she said. 'If you hadn't been phoning every day, if you'd given me even a bit of space! You were like a little kid. Want, want, want, all the time.'

'You should have said something. You've had me on your terms for weeks, and it's cruel. College was meant to be a new start, but since the first day I've just been hung up on you. So, did you plan to dump me before you left – or has this come on suddenly?'

'I never wanted to *dump* you. The last few weeks, I just hoped things would break off naturally with us at different places, meeting new people, and then we could stay friends, without all this awkwardness. But you never picked up on any of my hints.'

'Not returning my calls was deliberate?'

'I was hoping you'd get the message!'

'Charming!'

'I'm sorry! I just wanted to avoid telling you like this.'

I looked into her eyes. 'Did you ever love me? Were you lying when you said you did? *I* wouldn't say something like that unless I meant it. If you never liked me, why did you go out with me in the first place?'

'I did like you! You were shy and funny and completely different to my last boyfriend and I enjoyed giving you confidence—'

'So we were all about *you*. You feeling good for turning the ugly duckling into a swan.' Freya bit her lower lip, and I knew I was right. 'Christ, why didn't I realize? I really am thick. All you care about is yourself!'

'That's unfair! I never faked anything. I've put a lot into this relationship—'

'Only when it suited you.'

'My God, you have to analyse everything, don't you? Stop pushing this! I'm starting to say things I'll regret. Why are you making this so difficult?'

'Because it is!'

'I won't have you making me feel bad,' Freya snapped. 'I let this drag on for too long, and I was wrong not to tell you straight. Apart from that, I have nothing to apologize for.'

'Aren't you going to apologize for breaking my heart?'

'Oh, spare me the melodrama! For all you go on about me being selfish, it's clear all you care about is how much you're hurting. If you think about it, you'll realize your heart isn't broken at all.'

'That's crap!'

'Why did you ask me out in the first place?'

I paused. 'What do you mean? You know why.'

'Because you like being seen with me.'

'Rubbish! I like you for you—'

'You like me for the idea of me.'

I shook my head. 'Fine, if that's what you want to think. I know what I feel about you, Freya. This relationship means the world to me.'

'Relationship? We had a good time and made some great music, but it wasn't this amazing passionate romance – really it wasn't.'

'Well, that's how I saw it!'

'Broken record, Jonathan!' Freya yelled, slapping her hands over her ears. 'All I want is to *live* a little! What you need to understand is that a relationship should be *fun*. It isn't a matter of life and death.'

I didn't care how loudly I was shouting now. 'Well, maybe it is, actually, because right now I might just go and kill myself!'

Freya froze, then drew herself up straight. 'You wouldn't have the guts.'

'Try me. I'll jump under a train. It'll be all your fault.'

'You know what you are, Jonathan? Really immature.' Freya thrust an arm towards the door. 'I don't have to listen to this crap. I want you to leave, now. Go on, get out!'

'You know what you are, Freya? A heartless, selfish, two-faced bitch.'

'*Get out!*'

I flung the door open. Freya's eavesdropping friends had to skip back quickly. As I stalked out, I heard Freya scream, 'Everyone leave me alone!' and the slam of her door made the overhead light in the hallway rattle.

Exactly what happened next was a bit of a blur. Anger consumed me and I lost track of time – I remember running, but not much else. It felt like I was burning up with rage: rage at Freya for all she'd said and at myself for not being clearer about how I felt. When I finally cooled down I found that I was by the river, quite near to Auntie Phil's. I stopped under a bridge and, back to the wall, slid down into a sitting position.

Freya had actually broken up with me and I didn't understand why. It wasn't for a good reason – like some guy she liked better waltzing on to the scene. It felt like we'd been part of a play, acting out a script that had gone terribly wrong.

I took out my phone. **My life is crap**, I texted Ros. **Might as well not bother any more.**

My body was starting to feel numb, so I moved on. By the time I'd got on the underground, my anger at Freya had flipped to horror. What on earth would I do without her? She was part of me. I had the photo of us from the school cabaret on my wall. Whenever I was feeling bad it cheered me up, because it proved I wasn't a loser – out of all the guys in the school, she'd chosen me. Our names sounded good together, we looked good together, we *were* good together. Even my parents said so – oh, God, Mum and Dad! They'd be devastated – they liked Freya so much.

I got off the train at Earl's Court – I could change on to the dark blue line here. That would take me to Leicester Square, the heart of London, where there'd be people, and places open 24/7. I'd spend the night wandering around. My parents wouldn't know – they thought I was with Freya. I hurt far too much to face them right now.

Rosalind
10.30 p.m.

My life is crap. Might as well not bother any more.

What are you supposed to do when you get a text like that?

There was only one thing I could think of that would have made Jonathan say this. Something had to have happened with Freya – maybe even a break-up! I felt a shiver of excitement, though I knew it was terrible of me.

wots up? I texted back.

Minutes passed. I swivelled round in my chair. Why was

he texting me rather than emailing or IMing? He was always online Saturday nights unless he was with Freya, which far as I knew he wasn't.

After fifteen minutes I sent another message. He didn't reply.

I could have just left it – he knew where I was if he wanted to talk. But I was worried now. I knew I wouldn't be able to get any sleep until I heard from him. For the first time I felt annoyed with Jonathan: it was unfair to put me in this position. I also wasn't sure I wanted another long conversation – Jonathan could be quite emotionally draining when he was upset. But he'd been great when I needed support, so I guessed we balanced each other out.

I could phone. I had his home number as well as his mobile. But I hate ringing people up – there's just something about it that makes me feel uncomfortable. Jonathan wasn't exactly a stranger, but he hadn't heard my voice and I was nervous I'd say something stupid. Online I had a chance to think out things that would sound mature, but on the phone he might twig my real age.

'Hi, thanks for calling.' Jonathan's voice came over his mobile's answerphone. 'I'm out zapping Daleks right now, but if I survive, I'll be sure to give you a call when I'm back in the TARDIS.' I couldn't see the point in leaving a message, so I rang off. Could I call him at home? It was half past ten – a little late, but I'd have to risk it.

'Hello?' said a female voice. Probably his mum – who didn't even know I existed.

'Hi,' I mumbled. 'Can I speak to Jonathan?'

'I'm afraid he's not here. Can I ask who's calling?'

'Just a friend,' I said quickly. 'Has he gone to London to see Freya?'

'Yes . . .' Jonathan's mum sounded wary now and I put the phone down quickly. Sometimes I wondered if I'd got in too deep for my own good.

Come on! I thought, staring at my mobile. Please let me know you're OK.

Jonathan
11.25 p.m.

At Leicester Square station, one thought crossed my mind: so many people. There was someone thrusting a leaflet in my face, laughing groups outside theatres and people pushing on to the road, unperturbed by the buses and taxis. A woman brushed past, almost knocking me down the station steps.

I walked to the square itself. I'd last been here a couple of years ago and it hadn't changed – cinemas, huge neon signs and a little park in the centre. I started to feel better as I slouched around. At home a kid out alone would have attracted attention, but here no one noticed me at all. I let go of my anxiety and allowed my legs to take me where they wanted, not really thinking of anything . . .

I snapped out of it when someone banged into me. Hands clamped on my shoulders, pushing me against a wall.

'Get out of my way, you little shit!'

I gasped, coming to with a start. A frightening-looking guy with a skull tattoo on the side of his head stood right in front of me, face twisted with anger. Survival instinct kicked in and I bolted. The man stepped forward as though he was going to pursue me, but changed his mind and shouted abuse instead. I turned a corner and weaved through some back roads until I felt safe. Panting, I found my way back to the main square, trying to catch my breath.

In just ten or fifteen minutes, everything had changed. The nicely dressed theatregoers had gone. In their place were people like the guy who'd banged into me. They hung around in groups, talking too loudly; some wore jeans that were falling apart, others had weird piercings and tattoos and one even had a dangerous-looking chain slung from his denim jacket. Their faces looked rough and hardened; I didn't need to get close to smell the alcohol. There were also tired-looking homeless people. One, a teenager, made me feel particularly uncomfortable. She had filthy hair and lay on her side in a sleeping bag, muttering to herself. I avoided meeting her eyes. Suddenly I was all too aware people were watching me. London was theirs now, and they knew I didn't belong . . .

Even with my coat, I was beginning to shiver. How had I thought traipsing round a city I didn't know alone at night was clever? I headed back the way I'd come, towards the station, my heart beating faster and faster.

It was closed.

I stood looking at the mesh barrier. I felt very sick indeed.

The last tube had gone. That meant the overground trains would have finished too.

Suddenly more than anything I wanted to be home.

My first thought was to call Ros. But when I took out my phone, it was dead. The battery had been low when I'd set out, I remembered. There would be a phone booth somewhere, but I didn't remember Ros's number, and she'd probably be asleep anyway. For a second I considered ringing home, but – God – Mum and Dad would hit the roof if they knew I was out at this hour. I was on my own.

Where could I go? There were pubs and bars open, but they would be packed with the kind of people I wanted to avoid. Stations? I bet Liverpool Street would be open, even if no trains were running – and at least I'd be in the right place for getting home when they did start. Maybe I could get a night bus there. Freya had been enthusing about those, saying how amazing it was that in London you could go anywhere at any time. I turned to check the tube map pinned outside the station and found myself staring at the bus map next to it.

Though all I wanted was to get away, I took my time. One bus seemed to go where I needed, so I set off to find the stop, trying to look as sorted as I could. After what seemed a very long fifteen minutes, the bus arrived. I thought the driver gave me a look when I got on, but he didn't say anything. I sat as close to the front as I could, partly because there was noise coming from the top deck and partly because I felt safer near the driver.

Liverpool Street was impossible to miss – but there was a mesh gate over the entrance. I went up and rattled it, but I could tell it wouldn't shift. Stupid me – why the hell had I assumed it would be open? They probably had to close it for cleaning – I could vaguely hear the hum of a sweeper.

Keep calm, I told myself, though I'd never felt closer to panicking. I walked round the side of the station to see if I could get in through another entrance. They were all shut – but next to one was a 24-hour McDonald's.

Relief flowed over me as I stepped inside and smelt the familiar frying smell. I was afraid I might attract attention, but the bored-looking man at the counter gave me a hot chocolate and burger without saying a word. I went up to the second floor. There were a couple of trampy guys picking at fries, but otherwise it was deserted. I made sure I sat as far away from them as I could. My burger was soggy but I was so hungry I didn't care; it was gone in a couple of mouthfuls. Cupping my hands round the hot-chocolate cup and feeling the warmth returning to my fingers, I rested my head against the wall.

It seemed a lifetime ago that I'd been in Freya's room, yelling at her. But when my mind slid back a year, and I saw all the things we'd done together and remembered the way she used to look at me, I realized that time had actually gone too quickly.

It felt as if I sat in McDonald's forever. A few people came and went – from their clothes I guessed they'd come from clubs and bars. At about half three, when I was starting to doze off, a woman started cleaning tables. 'You all right?' she said as she approached me.

She was an older woman; something about her reminded me of Mum. Quickly I said, 'Yeah, fine.'

'Sure you're not lost or something? You look a bit young to be here on your own.'

I shook my head. She gave me a long look, then turned and went downstairs. I hesitated a moment, then scrambled up. The woman obviously didn't believe me – she might be calling security, even the police. I didn't think it was a good idea to wait around and see what happened.

Outside, I saw that the grilles over the station entrances had been lifted. Cautiously I entered. It felt eerie, like a ghost station, lights on, but nobody home – no one, that was, apart from a guy slumped by WHSmith, head in a McDonald's bag. Wonder if his burger's soggy too, I thought, then jumped as a figure in uniform came into view. A security guard. I headed away, ducking behind pillars.

For the next hour I played cat and mouse with him. Then I found the toilets. I thought I might be able to hide until morning, but I had company. There were three guys standing by the hand dryers. Their eyes followed me as I stepped into a cubicle. I could hear someone nearby talking in a foreign language, and the air tasted stale and made me feel dizzy. I was afraid to go out so I stayed where I was, hunching on the toilet and pulling my knees to my chest.

Someone banged on the door. I jumped, almost falling off the seat, and tensed for whatever was coming next. But for some reason they lost interest in me, and I heard footsteps moving away. Deciding it was now or never, I unlocked the door and bolted out.

Once out, I slumped down in a corner. All I wanted was to go home and get out of this hell.

Sundays always seem slow to get going, but this one was something else. Sometime after seven people started trickling into the station. Thank God, I thought. Despite not sleeping, I didn't feel tired – just empty. I wandered up and down the concourse in zombie mode until the coffee stands opened. The woman at the AMT was the same one who'd been there when I'd been waiting for Ros. She smiled at me.

'Hey, I remember you – d'you always meet your mates here?'

I ordered a coffee and handed her a tenner.

'Don't have change for that. Got anything smaller?'

I shook my head. She pushed the coffee across the counter.

'Ah, have it for free. My boss'll never know. You look as though you could do with some caffeine.'

I took it, mumbling my thanks and turning away. I could feel moisture in my eyes.

I was the first person through the barrier when it opened for the 8.30 train to Norwich, the earliest of the day. I found a seat, leaned my head against the window and closed my eyes. I'd have to phone home at the other end – Mum and Dad would know something was wrong the moment they saw me, but I didn't care. I didn't care about anything . . .

Rosalind
Sunday 19 October, 5.50 p.m.

Jonathan appeared online late on Sunday afternoon.

that really u? I asked.

Yeah.

u ok? ur txt freaked me out!

Sorry.

wot happened?!

It was Freya, of course. He was so upset, and all I wanted to say was that if she could treat him like that then he was well rid of her. I didn't, of course. My role was to sympathize as he spewed out anger and hurt and tell him what he wanted to hear – that Freya might change her mind. He told me she was selfish and manipulative but in the same breath said he loved her. I didn't understand. Perhaps he was in denial, maybe he was panicking, possibly he really meant it. I wasn't sure and I don't think he knew either.

After we'd been talking two hours, I said, ***this is silly. il give u a call. promise 2 pick up the landline?***

OK.

I went through to the sitting room. Dad and Olivia were out, so there was no one to overhear.

'Hey.' Jonathan picked up instantly.

'Hi.' My voice wobbled a little. 'It's Ros. But you knew that.'

'Wow. You sound kinda like I expected. When you didn't show up that time I started to wonder if you really were who you said.'

'Then why did you keep emailing?'

I could almost see him shrug. 'Missed you.' And then he launched into telling me once again how he kept trying to ring Freya and apologize for shouting at her. He'd analysed every word of their argument and was even listening to a playlist that made him think of her. I started wondering if he needed proper help – something more than talking to me.

'I don't know what I'm going to do without her,' he said. 'She made me who I am.'

'You'll get past this,' I said. 'You're a great guy.'

'Doesn't feel that way.'

'You're funny. You give good advice. You're generous. You play the guitar really well –'

'You've never heard me.'

'Give me a break, Jono! Why are you always determined to look on the bad side?'

There was a pause. 'Sorry.'

'No, I'm sorry. Thing is . . .' I hesitated. 'I know what it's like to have everything fall apart and blame yourself. I don't want you to go through that.'

'This is about your mum, right?'

'Yeah.' I closed my eyes. 'She began a part-time university degree when I was in Year 5. It was something she'd always wanted to do. Mum had odd parents and had kids young because she wanted to prove to them she'd grown up and could run her own life. Dad thought the degree was great; he didn't go to uni either, and he's always in awe of smart people. But she got more and more into it, especially after meeting the other students, and history of art wasn't something Dad or Olivia or me could share with her.'

'Didn't she make time for you?'

'At first. But she started resenting us and feeling tied down. If she hadn't had a family, she could have gone to uni and got a great job.'

'But she chose that.'

I shrugged. 'We got the blame.'

'So she walked out?'

'Dad met her friends but he didn't fit in. There were arguments, and one day there was a really bad one and she left.'

'I don't see how this is your fault.'

I couldn't stop myself sounding bitter. 'Me and Olivia weren't good enough for her to stay, were we?'

Jonathan paused. I got the impression he might not know what to say. 'Do you see her any more?'

'Couldn't at first. She went to live abroad with some guy she met on her course. She phones and stuff, but it isn't the same. Apparently she's moving back soon, but I don't want to see her. She tossed me out of her life – why should I keep her in mine? And I hope she's hurt. I've hurt all the times I wanted her and she wasn't there.'

'Not trying to defend her, but she probably didn't think things through. People don't when they really want something.'

'Well, she *should* have thought. She should have been less selfish.'

'Are you crying, Ros?'

I rubbed at my eyes. 'Kind of. I just realized that despite everything, I miss her. Doesn't make sense, does it? Just . . . I remember what she was like. I loved that mum. Pretending she's become someone completely different doesn't work.'

I was thinking of Brighton. A year before everything went wrong we went there on a day trip. It was one of those perfect family days you always remember. When we arrived Olivia and I nearly cried because the beach wasn't sandy, but Mum turned it around by drawing faces on the pebbles and making this amazing game out of them. We had chips for lunch, two ice creams, and we went on a roller coaster on the pier – it was the first time I'd been on such a scary ride and I was so excited! – and we even stayed on for a firework display in the evening, which was amazing. Thinking of Brighton made me feel sick. Mum had been so good at making things fun – and she'd always been the one who was interested in my artwork too, cutting out paper dolls for me to colour and later on tearing interesting pictures from her magazines for me to work from. How had it got to the point where I didn't even want to talk to her any more?

'I feel crap now,' Jonathan said. 'Every time I think I've got it bad, you come out with something worse.'

'Didn't mean to make you feel crap.' I pulled a tissue from the box on the coffee table. 'I've never really talked to anyone about this – it runs a bit too deep. I mean, me and

Olivia used to, but we don't have much to do with each other these days. She's always busy.'

'I sort of understand.'

'How? You have two parents who love you.'

He paused. 'Mum and Dad are older than most parents of sixteen-year-olds. I'm the kid they didn't think they were going to have – and that brings a ton of pressure with it. I have to do well at everything and be better than everyone else – they push me so much academically. Trying hard all the time gets to you after a while.'

'You got the best GCSE results in your school – I bet they're really proud of you.'

'Yeah, but for every good there's a bad. Some really bad.'

'Really bad?'

'Something happened back in February with a guy called Tom Copeland. I lost my temper, he ended up in hospital, the police got involved and it was a real mess.'

'Wow. What did you do to him?'

A pause. 'Don't want to talk about it.'

My eyes widened. 'OK. You know I'm here if you do.'

'Uh-huh. Thanks, Ros. You're a good mate.'

It was a compliment, but it didn't make me smile. 'I phoned last night, you know. I was worried.'

'Mum said a girl had rung.'

'Sorry.'

'Nah, I'm sorry. Unfair of me to send that text at all, but

I wasn't thinking straight.' He sighed. 'I'm in the doghouse at the moment.'

'About last night?'

'Mum keeps saying that anything could have happened to me, wandering the streets at night. Guess she's right.' He let out a half-hearted laugh. 'Good thing Freya dumped me and Mum and Dad feel they have to be sympathetic, else I'd be getting it worse than this.'

'What did your parents say about Freya?'

'Lots of stuff about how everything ends sooner or later and maybe we were growing apart anyway – like they know! Dad tried to tell me about a girl who dumped him back in the Dark Ages – it was really awkward.' Jonathan paused. 'Dunno how things will be with Dad now. He respected me when Freya was around. It was a kind of "my son has a girlfriend, he's normal after all" kind of thing. Think he might've thought I was gay before.'

'What? Why?'

'Dad's a bit old-fashioned. In his book, blokes play sport, not muck about with computers.'

'I think you're unfair on your parents. Sure, you don't see eye to eye, but it sounds like they're both there for you.'

'True. Guess I should be grateful, after what you said about your mum. Puts it in perspective.'

'If you look hard enough you'll see that the world's not that much worse because Freya dumped you. Like my dad says sometimes, with every end comes a new beginning.'

'I don't see that.'

'Well,' I said, trying to sound casual, 'you might meet someone else.'

'Don't want anyone else. When you love someone, you can't just turn those feelings off.'

Don't I know it, I thought. Once more, Hugh's words played on my mind: 'Love tells you who you are.'

Jonathan
Friday 24 October, 10.00 a.m.

'Please talk to me.' I'd lost track of the number of times I'd left Freya voicemail now. 'I said cruel things I didn't mean and I'm sorry. Stop blanking me and call back – please?'

By the end of the week I decided I had to go and see her again. I was missing classes, but I didn't care. On the train I found an abandoned London paper and flicked through it. SECOND GIRL MISSING: POLICE SUSPECT LINK WITH THAMES MURDER, cried the headline. *Concern is growing for Lyndsey Brown, 17, last seen in the Hammersmith area late on 27 September . . . Lyndsey hasn't been home since the start of August.* A photograph of a black-haired girl with lots of jewellery accompanied the article. I hoped she wasn't going to end up like the other missing girl Freya had told me about.

When I arrived at Auntie Phil's no one answered. I was about to try phoning again when I spotted one of the girls who'd been in the kitchen the night Freya dumped me walking past. I caught up with her.

'Hi. Do you know where Freya is?'

The girl gave me a dirty look. 'No, and I wouldn't tell you if I did. She was in tears after you left last Saturday. Screaming at everyone to leave her alone.'

'Look, I just want to talk to her. Maybe I should try the conservatoire.'

'Don't bother. She hasn't been in all week.'

'How come?'

'Dunno. I live across the road – haven't seen anyone going in or out the house either. Maybe she's been ill.'

'When was the last time you did see her?'

'Saturday – when you were here. We ended up going to the club without her. She went out shortly after we did though. My parents saw her leave.'

'What? You mean she went out alone, five days ago, and you haven't seen her since?'

'Uh-huh. No idea where she was going.'

'And you haven't contacted the police?'

She looked as me as though I was from another planet. 'Why would I?'

'A girl a few streets away was strangled last month! There's someone else missing now and she's from south London too – haven't you seen the news?' The blank look on her face infuriated me, and I raised my voice. 'Freya could have been abducted! If there's some sicko watching for lone girls, she'd have been a prime target! And if she hasn't been seen for days . . .'

'Don't yell at me. I haven't done anything.'

'Have you spoken to her mates? Has anyone heard from her?'

'How should I know? Look, there's bound to be an explanation for this. It's nothing to get worked up about.'

'One girl's dead, another's missing and that's "nothing"? Are you thick or something?'

She gave me a disgusted look and started walking more quickly. I let her go; I was already heading back to Auntie Phil's. Checking no one was watching, I felt through the bush by the door. My fingers brushed a plastic bag – and in it a key, just like Freya had said.

Inside, the house was dark and silent. Post lay on the doormat. I placed it on the table by the door. In the kitchen unwashed dishes were stacked in the sink, including the wok from Saturday night. Upstairs, in Freya's room, I found the curtains closed, the lamp on – and her mobile still on the table. The screen was blank – the battery had worn down.

I felt sick. Freya wasn't the kind of girl to go anywhere without her phone.

Rosalind
1.00 p.m.

Abby and I were hanging out round the back of the art block at lunchtime. She was filling me in on how things were going with Brian, whom she'd met several times since our trip to Gabe's house. They'd done a lot of kissing, and Abby thought he was fantastic – real boyfriend material. Apparently he liked her too; never wanted her to leave when she went round, said she was beautiful, gave her loads of the jewellery he'd made. I didn't talk about Jonathan much now; Abby knew I'd explained my no-show to him and that we were talking again, but making up nice things he'd said to me didn't feel good any more. I was almost sorry half-term was starting tomorrow; at least school was a distraction. The only plus was that Dad had decided to go to Paris with Petra after all.

When my mobile buzzed I thought I was imagining it. No one had ever called me at school before. My heart quickened when I saw who it was.

'Keep a lookout for teachers,' I said to Abby, then picked up, trying to sound normal. 'Hey. What's up?'

'Freya's disappeared,' said Jonathan. 'She went off by herself last Saturday and no one's seen her since. This is totally unlike her.'

'She's still not returning calls?' I asked.

'Her phone's still in her room. Couldn't find her purse though, so hopefully she has cash . . . I'm on the green underground line heading to the conservatoire to check she isn't there. Maybe I should call the police – I keep thinking about that dead girl—'

'Calm down, Jono. Why don't you call her friends first – and her parents. She might be staying with them.'

'I can't call her parents – they'd give me an earful! Maybe I can talk to one of her neighbours back home, or something. And I can't calm down! If something's happened it's my fault because I made her get upset and run off, don't you see? She always has waitressing shifts on Fridays – maybe I can catch her at the restaurant, though I don't have a clue where it is – Hey, Ros? You know London better than I do. Maybe you could give me a hand?'

My eyes widened. 'What? Now?'

'Yeah, any chance of you skipping school? I could really do with having a friend around right now.'

I pictured him, nervy and probably not thinking straight. Of all the people he could have called for help, he had picked me. 'OK. We'll meet at Embankment station in an hour. That's near the music school, right?'

'Yeah. Thanks, Ros. See you soon.'

I ended the call. Abby reached up and poked my cheek. 'You've gone pale.'

'Jonathan's in London,' I said. 'His friend's disappeared

and he's worried sick.' Snapping into action, I took out my purse. Thankfully Abby and I had been planning to go to the cinema after school and I'd slipped in a few quid this morning. I had just enough for a travel card.

Abby was gazing at me with a funny expression on her face. 'You're bunking off school.'

'He asked me. I can't say no – God, Abby, how do I even get out?'

'Claudia,' Abby said.

We found her round by the Portakabins having a secret smoke.

'Ros needs to bunk,' said Abby. 'What's the best way?'

Claudia took a slow drag then threw the stub on to the ground, grinding it with her heel.

Infuriated I snapped, 'There's only ten minutes of break left!'

'You don't want to piss me off or I might not help.' Claudia gave me a catty smile.

I took a steadying breath. 'Sorry.'

'You need someone to distract the dinner staff. Best way out is the east entrance cos you can creep behind the bushes.'

'How do I do that?'

'You bribe my little brother and his mates.' Coolly Claudia held out a hand. I looked pleadingly at Abby. She dug through her bag and found her cinema money. Claudia counted the coins then pocketed them.

'Go to the east entrance and wait out of sight. When a Year 7 yells that someone's been hurt playing footie, you get out.'

'Thanks.' Feeling grateful to Claudia – now, there was a new sensation! – Abby and I went to the east entrance and hovered just out of sight of the teacher on duty.

'I don't understand,' Abby hissed. 'I thought you were afraid of meeting Jonathan.'

'I am, but if we do this now, when he needs me, maybe my appearance won't matter and he'll see me in a different light–'

'Mrs Sanders!' A boy ran out from the path to the games area. 'Rory's had an accident.'

The teacher took off as fast as she could, and I made for the bushes. As I crept through I was sure that any moment a window would shoot open and a teacher would yell my name. I kept under cover as long as I could before bolting through the gates on to the road. I didn't stop running until I was sure I was out of sight. Then, checking no one was about, I took off my school tie and stuffed it in my bag.

This was the last thing I needed – why had I been stupid enough to say yes? I untucked my shirt and undid the top two buttons. There wasn't much I could do with my blazer, so I left it as it was. I considered rolling up my skirt a few inches like many of my classmates did, but decided the less of my legs that showed the better. Wishing I had a mirror,

I raked a hand through my hair but soon realized it was no good. When I met Jonathan, I would look my ordinary, childish self and there was nothing I could do about it.

He was waiting by the ticket machines at Embankment.

It'll be OK, I kept telling myself. He won't care about the lies . . .

His eyes were glued on the station clock. He was dressed almost identically to how he had been in that first photograph, looking cool and grown-up. Dragging out my steps, I went up to him.

He glanced round as I approached, taking in my presence before looking back at the clock. I took a breath.

'Hi. I'm Ros.'

His head turned slowly. He stared at me.

7. Away

Jonathan
2.00 p.m.

Suddenly there was this kid standing next to me. If she hadn't been wearing a skirt I might have mistaken her for a boy. She was clutching her rucksack strap so hard that her knuckles were white. In the midst of the office staff on their lunch break she looked little and lost.

'Hi. I'm Ros,' the kid said.

My mind flipped back to the two girls in the photograph. One was pretty, with long hair and trendy clothes and a great figure. The other was boyish, maybe about thirteen, and I hadn't given her a second glance.

'I'm sorry I lied to you.'

I realized I was staring and looked away.

'Ros? How old are you?' I asked.

'Fourteen.' There was a pause. 'And a half.'

God. I'd been confiding my thoughts in a child.

'I didn't think you'd want to speak to me if I told you who I really was,' she said.

I paced round in a circle, blowing out a long breath.

'You wouldn't have, right?' Rosalind asked.

I glanced at her. It was eerie to hear the voice I'd

associated with the glamorous girl coming out of her little sister's mouth. 'You've bunked off.'

She nodded. 'You asked me to.'

'You should get back.'

'But I'm here now,' she said. 'We're going to find Freya.'

'Is this why you didn't show up the last time? Because you're – you?'

Another nod.

'Why did you lie? I was just some random guy when I first spoke to you.'

'I dunno.' She looked really embarrassed. 'I guess – well, you said stuff that made me think. No one's ever given me advice like that before, 'specially not a boy. Then you made me laugh – we liked the same TV shows – and I needed a friend.' She pressed her lips together, eyes flicking away for a moment. 'I'm the same person I was online and on the phone. The only difference is, you can see my face. I know I'm not pretty like my sister.'

'It's not the way you look that bothers me,' I said. 'It's just that – well, there are things I maybe wouldn't have said if I'd known you were fourteen.'

'But you did, and you never knew the difference,' she said softly. 'There's only two years between us – that's nothing.'

Rosalind was looking at the ground, shoulders hunched, and I suddenly felt sorry for her. Maybe I shouldn't blame her for lying. After all, I knew what it was like to be lonely.

'Look – Rosalind – we could talk about this for hours,' I said, 'but I've got to find Freya. If you don't fancy going back to school, you might as well come along and show me how to get around London. Maybe we can work something out as we go.'

She nodded and we walked in silence to the escalators.

Rosalind
2.10 p.m.

How small is it possible to feel before you disappear?

I felt childish.

I felt ugly.

I felt like a fool for playing at being someone I wasn't.

And after all we'd shared online, we had nothing to say apart from stupid stranger talk. I explained about underground lines, in more detail than he needed because I was afraid of silence. Jonathan listened politely and offered me the only spare seat when we got into a carriage, perhaps to get me out of the way because I was embarrassing him. We called each other 'Rosalind' and 'Jonathan' rather than 'Ros' and 'Jono'. It was as though we'd never spoken.

I felt like crying, but I didn't because I knew it was my fault.

We got off at Richmond. Jonathan's trip to the conservatoire had drawn a blank, and he wanted to check Freya's room again. I pretended not to know where we were going as we headed to Ridgemont Street.

'You know,' Jonathan said, 'what actually surprises me most is you're really short. I was picturing you being taller.'

I could tell he was trying to be friendly, but it wasn't helping. I played along anyway. 'Really? I was picturing you being shorter.'

He gave me a lopsided, unconvincing smile. I mimicked it, and pretended it made everything all right.

Jonathan took a key from the bush outside the house and let us in.

''S'OK,' he said, reading the look on my face. 'Her aunt's on holiday.'

I hovered on the doorstep, taking in the clean, cream-coloured carpet, the framed photographs on the wall, the coats neatly hung up to my left. This was Freya's house, Freya's life. I wondered what would happen if she suddenly came back and found me inside; me, the kid who'd stalked her.

'Rosalind?' Jonathan was halfway up the stairs. 'Come on.'

I shook my head. 'Can't. Feels wrong.'

'It's fine – no one will even know. It's not like we're going to nick anything.'

Even though I'd never touched any of Freya's things, somehow it felt like I'd stolen from her already. But I didn't have much choice, unless I wanted to hang around outside. I stepped in, telling myself I was doing this for Jonathan.

Freya's room was small and square, the walls covered by posters and photographs. The bed was unmade, and there were clothes everywhere, piled on a spare chair, a shelf, the top of the chest of drawers.

By the bed lay something red and silky. Unable to resist, I picked it up. It was a nightie – the sexy kind Abby and I admired through the windows of underwear shops. I felt slightly sick. Of course Freya would have one. I wondered if Jonathan had bought it for her.

'Maybe she *didn't* plan to get rid of me before she came to London.' Jonathan was standing by the window. In his hand he held a stuffed white rabbit with a pink bow round its neck. I dropped the nightie quickly.

'What makes you think that?'

He waved the rabbit at me. 'Gave her this on Valentine's Day. Thought it was sweet – a bunny from Squeebunny. She gave me the nickname, you know. I hated it at first, but it ended up sticking.'

'Oh. Right.'

'I know it's only a cuddly toy, but it's special. Back home she kept it on her pillow, and she even took it into exams with her as a mascot. Why would she bring it here if she didn't care about me any more?'

The rabbit stared at us with blank, happy eyes, and I looked away.

'I don't know.'

Jonathan wiggled the rabbit's ears. 'Squee,' he said flatly, and put it down. He wandered over to look at the photographs on one of the walls. I didn't want to look, but I found myself joining him. Some seemed older than others; one showed Freya at maybe my age, posing behind a birthday cake with her parents. Even then she looked great; I wondered if she had ever known what it was like to feel awkward in her body or have a crush on someone who didn't like her back. I doubted it.

There were also a lot of photos of the stuffed bunny.

'It's just a daft thing we do,' Jonathan said. 'It was Freya's idea – she's a real shutterbug. We take photos of it in strange places. Like, once we sneaked into the head teacher's room at school and snapped it sitting on his chair.'

I felt a bit of a pang. He was still so deeply attached to Freya.

'There are some nice photos of you here,' I said.

'Wouldn't call them nice. I'm not very photogenic.'

'You look different without your glasses.' I pointed to one in which he appeared to be asleep, the bunny peeping out from under the bedclothes beside him. Jonathan made a face.

'Yuck.'

'Where was it taken?'

'Edinburgh. My aunt and uncle live there and said we could come up for a holiday after our GCSEs. They weren't about so it was just the two of us. Freya woke up early one morning and thought it'd be fun to take embarrassing pictures of me.'

'Oh. Were your parents OK with that?'

'What, going to Edinburgh?' He gave me a funny look. 'Course.'

Argh! Why did I have to ask stupid, childish questions? They'd have been sixteen – old enough to be independent and do what they wanted. Old enough to share a bed.

Jonathan didn't notice that I was blushing. 'It was a really great week. I know I go on about her, but Freya's fun, especially when you get her alone. We saw loads of sights and mucked about at the castle pretending to be pirates – dunno why, but it made sense at the time. The best bit was the last two days. We'd spent all our money and ended up wandering around the city and just talking. For the first time I felt someone understood me. Maybe I'm being OTT, but that holiday's the only time I've ever felt truly happy.'

Now I felt even more uncomfortable. Even though they were only photographs, I felt like I was nosing into Jonathan and Freya's special moments. Me, who had never had a boyfriend or even been kissed, and spent far too much time wondering what it was like.

'Maybe we ought to do what we came here to do,' I said. Jonathan nodded. He went over to Freya's laptop, lifting the cover. Very gingerly I perched on the desk beside him.

'What time is Freya due at the restaurant?'

'Around six, I'd guess. If she's not there, I'll panic. Not turning up for classes is one thing – Freya's skived before – but work is another. She's always skint.'

He clicked on the Internet browser and typed in the URL to a webmail site. Seeing the address he entered, I said, 'You're looking at her email?'

'I know her password; she might have emailed someone saying where she is. I can't believe I didn't think of this earlier! At the very least, if she's sent anything since Saturday it'll tell me she's OK.'

I thought of how I would feel if someone found their way into my account and read my messages, and squirmed. 'This isn't a good idea,' I said, but Jonathan wasn't listening. Freya's inbox popped up. The first ten emails were all from the same address. Jonathan clicked on the latest, sent last Friday – several hours before Freya had dumped him. I read it over his shoulder – and felt sorrier and sorrier for him as it became clear what kind of email it was.

Jonathan
3.05 p.m.

'Just as I thought this couldn't get any worse . . .' I stared at the screen, feeling the colour drain from my face.

From: 'H_A_Clark@hotmail.co.uk'
To: 'Freya Rose'
Date: Friday 17 October, 19:37

Bonjour la fille magnifique!

Obviously you're bored in class again if you're sending me suggestive texts. Bet you haven't got any work done this morning, bad girl. Meet six o'clock at the usual place? And before you ask, no, I will not tell you what I have planned, even if you beg. It is a surprise. ;)

By the way, there is a dress in the window of a charity shop round mine you would adore. Fancy a late birthday present?
xxx
PS – You are absolutely beautiful.

'She's found someone else,' I said.

'Sorry,' Rosalind said in a small voice.

I clicked on another message, snorting as I read the first line. 'The bloke's an idiot; what kind of person addresses emails "Dear Goddess"?'

'It's Norse mythology. Freya's a goddess – of lust, actually.'

I clicked on the 'sent items' folder and opened Freya's response to the first message. When I saw there was an attachment, my heart stopped. It was a new photo of the bunny, balanced on the shoulder of a bemused-looking man in a fancy uniform.

'That's a beefeater,' Rosalind said. 'It's the Tower of London.'

I swallowed. 'I never saw this picture. Do you know what that means?'

'What?'

'She's been playing the bunny game with this bloke. It's ours – this daft little thing that no one else understands –' This hurt far more than I could say.

Here's Bunny sightseeing, Freya had written. *Next it's your turn to take her somewhere fun. I dare you to try the Houses of Parliament. Bunny's always wanted to meet the Prime Minister!*
F xxxxxxxxxxxxxxx
PS – My friend saw that text you sent me yesterday. She was shocked. :)

I scrolled down, feeling sick as flirty lines and nicknames jumped out at me. The new boyfriend seemed to know Freya pretty well for someone who'd presumably met her recently; worse, she obviously really liked him. She'd even sent across a few paragraphs from one of her favourite astrology websites: *See, Libra and Gemini are a perfect match!* In one email the bloke asked *So when are you dumping Jonny-boy?* This one didn't seem to have been answered; maybe just as well.

This is the last time I hack anyone's account, I thought. There are some things you just don't want to know.

Rosalind
3.10 p.m.

Jonathan turned from the screen looking utterly crushed. I fiddled with the hem of my skirt.

'So she hasn't sent any emails this week,' I said.

Jonathan sighed. 'No.'

'Maybe she's staying with him?'

He snorted. 'That would be classic. Break up with your boyfriend, then go to your new bloke for sympathy.'

'He didn't sign any emails, but the sender shows as H. A. Clark – know who that could be?'

'There was someone around the night Freya dumped me who blatantly fancied the pants off her. Name's Adam – maybe he goes by his middle name.'

'Guess it's worth checking. Is his number on her phone?'

'We'll have better luck finding her address book.' Jonathan rummaged in the desk drawer. 'Freya gives everyone daft nicknames on her phone.'

We found the address book. There were no guys listed under H – and he wasn't under C for Clark, either.

'Should've know it wouldn't be up to date,' Jonathan grumbled. 'There's a landline number for Adam though. Guess I should try that.' He entered the number into his phone and pressed dial.

'Hello, is Adam there?' He paused, presumably listening to the voice on the other end. 'Right. OK. Could you give me his mobile number? Look, it's really important.'

After a moment he cut the call, shaking his head. 'No go. His mum just got shirty with me.'

I pressed my lips together. 'Freya would have Adam's mobile number if they were going out.'

'Maybe this is all a wild goose chase.' Jonathan blew out a breath that made his fringe rise off his forehead. 'God, I should be mad at her, but I'm too worried. Just want to do something for her.'

Something that would persuade her to take him back, I thought. He wants her to be a damsel in distress so he can be the knight in shining armour.

If he had been anyone else I would have put an arm round him. As it was, I said, 'Talk to her friends.'

As soon as it turned half three, I slipped out and called Abby's mobile. Even though I was only on the street outside, it came as a relief to get out of the house.

'You got away then,' she said when she picked up. 'Did you meet him? Where are you?'

'We're at Richmond,' I said in a low voice. 'Did the teachers say anything about me?'

'They asked where you were; I said you had a dentist's appointment.'

'Thanks, Abby; I'll have to forge a note on Monday.'

'Ros . . . what's all this about? Are you OK?'

I sighed. 'It's complicated. Can I tell you later? Not a good time right now.'

'OK. Here if you need me.'

At half four, Jonathan put the address book down.

'Nothing,' he said. 'No one has a clue where she is.'

There was nothing on Freya's mobile either. Jonathan had found the charger and checked it, but all that showed on the phone were his calls and some unrelated texts from female friends.

I looked over from where I was sitting by the bed. 'Did

you try every single number?'

'The ones I could get through to.'

'What about her home? Maybe she went to see her parents.'

'I'm trying to get hold of a friend who lives a few doors down; Freya would kill me if I kicked up a fuss with her parents.'

'Do you want to go and wait for her at the restaurant?'

'Not much else to do, is there?'

We took the train up to Hammersmith, where we had to change. As we were early and Jonathan needed to buy more phone credit, we found a newsagent. When we returned to the station, it was teaming with activity and the trains were packed.

'Is it normally like this?' Jonathan asked as we squashed on to a carriage.

'At this time, always. People are getting home from work.' A businessman squeezed in just as the doors closed and I found myself pressed up against Jonathan. Oh, help – he's even better-looking up close, I thought, aware that I could feel his ribs. I didn't know where to look – if I glanced away it was as though I didn't want to be there, if I gazed straight ahead all I could see was his chest, and if I met his eyes I knew I would blush. In the end I moved my head so I could see over his shoulder.

'Hope you're not claustrophobic,' I said.

Out of the corner of my eye I saw him smile. 'Nope. Hope you took a shower this morning.'

I had to fight not to lean against him as the train gathered pace. I wanted so much to rest my head against his chest. Deciding I'd better concentrate on being practical, I said, 'We're on this line until Green Park, then we need to change.'

'I'll leave directions to you. I'm still pretty clueless – I'd only been to London a couple of times before Freya came here.'

'How do you like it?'

'London itself is great, but the underground does my head in. It's far simpler where I'm from – you get in the car and drive from A to B. First thing you do when you turn seventeen, learn to drive.'

I hadn't even thought about driving lessons yet. Turning seventeen seemed a long way off.

'While you were on the phone I did some thinking,' I said, taking care not to give away that I knew more about Freya than I was supposed to. 'Freya doesn't sound like the kind of girl to keep quiet when she's upset.'

'She yelled at her friends to go away – but I guess she might have been embarrassed. They overheard more or less everything.'

'So maybe she went to another friend. She'd be feeling bad and want to speak to someone who'd take her side and tell her she did the right thing. That may mean someone who doesn't know you.'

Jonathan tilted his head. 'Hmm. Reckon you have something there. Freya's a sucker for sympathy.'

I wasn't sure what to say to that, so I took out the mini *A–Z* I kept in my bag and showed Jonathan where Freya's restaurant was. He thanked me for being patient with him.

'You're really organized,' he added, and it wasn't just my imagination telling me he sounded impressed. 'Freya and me always got lost when we went new places. Her brain's cotton wool with directions and mine's not much better.'

'I just like to know where I am,' I said. 'Is it an Italian Freya works at? Sounds like it from the name.'

'Yup. Hungry?'

I glanced at my feet. 'Yeah, but I've no money on me.'

'I have.' Jonathan flashed one of his lopsided smiles at me. 'Fancy a bowl of spaghetti?'

As it happened we arrived before Freya was due, so we really did sit and eat spaghetti. The only problem was that it was quite pricey, so we ended up buying one bowl between us. Spaghetti's messy enough when it's your own, but sharing is a recipe for disaster. We kept flicking tomato sauce everywhere. Maybe because we were so tense, it all seemed very funny – especially when Jonathan said it reminded him of the famous scene in *Lady and the Tramp*.

'Good job we didn't order meatballs, else I'd have to push the last one across the plate towards you with my nose,' he said.

I giggled and was about to say that we'd better not both accidentally start eating the same strand of spaghetti when I heard someone say Freya's name. A man in a chef's jacket was talking to our waitress. She was shaking her head; the man walked back into the kitchen looking annoyed.

Jonathan caught the waitress's eye, and she came over.

'Has Freya arrived yet?' he asked. 'I'm her boyfriend and I need to have a word with her.'

'No, she's late, but that's nothing new.' The waitress looked him up and down curiously. 'And there was me thinking that other bloke was her boyfriend.'

'What other bloke?' said Jonathan instantly.

'Last couple of weeks a guy's been coming in every night Freya works. She's always wandering over to his table to chat.'

'What's he like?' I asked.

'Early twenties, longish dark hair, good-looking, bit scruffy. She wouldn't tell me anything, but I got the impression they were together.'

'When Freya comes in could you let me know?' said Jonathan. The waitress nodded and moved on. Jonathan circled his empty glass on the tabletop. 'Why do I even care? She's cheating on me, and yet I'm worried as hell about her.'

'Bit like me and my mum. You care because you can't pretend she didn't happen and you can't help how you feel.' And I could say the same about you, I thought sadly.

'I was wrong about that Adam. He isn't Freya's new boyfriend; doesn't fit the description. Christ, how many blokes has she been flirting with?'

'Dunno. If she turns up you can ask her.'

Jonathan grunted. 'Look, you should go home. Your dad'll be on the warpath soon.'

'It's OK. He's gone to Paris with Petra for a long weekend.'

'Everyone seems to be on holiday at the moment.'

'Well, it is half-term next week. Anyway, Olivia's in charge, but she's probably out with Mr Wonderful, so no one will care what I'm doing.' After hesitating a second, I placed my hand on his arm. 'This is the plan. We wait here a while. If she doesn't show, you come and stay at mine and we pick up the search tomorrow.'

'You sure?'

'Of course,' Even as I said it, I wondered what on earth I was doing. Olivia would be furious if I brought a strange boy home.

'Thanks. I don't fancy dragging myself all the way back. Oh, shit!' Jonathan gave a start. 'Never told my parents where I am. They'll be wondering why I haven't come home from college.' He fumbled with his phone. 'Hi,

Mum? It's me. Look, um, this is gonna sound odd, but I'm actually in London at the moment, so I'm not coming home tonight . . . What? . . . No, it's OK. I'm – I'm with Freya. We're working stuff out. Spur-of-the-moment kind of thing. No, won't go out alone again, promise. OK? Bye.'

He put the phone down, looking sheepish. 'They wouldn't like me staying with someone they don't know.'

It was odd seeing Jonathan get flustered about his parents. I'd always seen him as so grown-up, above that kind of thing.

It was half six now – and there was still no Freya. We waited until eight, checked with the waitress to see if she'd called, and, finding she hadn't, conceded defeat.

By the time we came out of West Finchley station it was half past nine. As we approached my road I said, 'Don't think Olivia will like me bringing you home, so when I open the door we're going to sneak right up to my room.'

Jonathan gave me a look and I felt more childish than ever. 'You said this was OK.'

'It is. Kind of.'

'Look, if this is a problem, Ros, I'll go.'

'We're here now.' The lights were on; Olivia was home after all. And judging by the noise, so were most of her friends.

I unlocked the front door. The hall was empty. The chatter and music came from the living room.

'Quick,' I pushed Jonathan forward. I hovered behind, preparing an excuse in case someone came out, but we made it to my room without seeing anyone.

'Dad told her no throwing parties,' I said, closing the door. 'At least I've got something I can use against her if she spots you.'

Jonathan kicked off his shoes, looking around. I felt oddly exposed as his eyes swept over my figurines and old teddies and bookshelves.

'Your room's very . . . girly,' he said. 'Didn't see you as a girly girl somehow.'

'It's only pink because pink was my favourite colour as a kid and Dad hasn't got round to redecorating.'

'Even Freya doesn't have a pink room.'

I wished he would stop mentioning her. 'Want something to eat? I know we had spaghetti, but that was a while ago. I could make more pasta – or a sandwich.'

'Either's fine, long as there's no celery in them. The canteen meals at sixth form – dunno why, but they've always got celery, whether it's curry or pizza or soup. Stuart reckons college owns a celery farm – Why the heck am I telling you this? What's wrong with me?'

'Calm down.' I pulled out the computer chair. He sat, not quite meeting my eyes.

'Sorry. Wouldn't be so worried if it wasn't for those two girls on the news.'

I shook my head. 'You're just being a good boyfriend.'

'I was dumped. Can't be that good a boyfriend.'

'Freya isn't right about everything,' I said.

He muttered something I didn't catch. Seeing my sketchbook on the desk I handed it over, though usually I hate showing people my pictures – there's a bit too much of me in them. 'You could look at this while I'm downstairs. Be right back.'

Jonathan
9.50 p.m.

I leaned back in the chair as Rosalind went out and I let out my breath slowly. What the hell was I doing in this pink room, with these ghastly china figurines of women in ball gowns? Today had started off like any other day – oversleeping, knocking my specs off the bedside table, nearly missing the zombie bus. Yet now Freya was cheating on me, had vanished and was maybe in a really bad place.

I flicked through the sketchbook. Ros was definitely talented, I thought, studying a portrait of an attractive woman I recognized from some film. No wonder she wanted to go to art college. I turned the page and found – myself. For a moment I was stunned by the likeness. Then I noticed that my hair was neater, my nose straighter, my cheekbones more pronounced.

'You've made me look like an action hero,' I said when Rosalind reappeared with a plate in each hand.

'Oh.' She sounded a little flustered. 'Here. Cheese and tomato.'

'It's awesome,' I said as I took the sandwich, 'but I'm not that good-looking.'

'I think you are.'

'Maybe if I ditched the specs and worked out, but right now, no way.'

'Don't you like your glasses? They're cool.'

'Freya chose them for me. Suppose they're OK, but they make me look like a cliché: speccy swot.'

'You should be proud of being clever.' Rosalind was nibbling off her sandwich crusts. 'All I'm good at is art.'

'Believe me, being top of the class hasn't done me much good. People take the mick out of you'

'When did you start playing the guitar?'

We talked about everything from music to her figurines. I was surprised by how quickly the time passed, and how easy it was to forget Ros was only fourteen. In a weird way I was reminded of how it had been at the beginning with Freya. We probably could have talked all night if I hadn't started feeling tired.

'You sleep here,' Ros said, getting up. 'I'll go in Dad's

room. I said goodnight to Livy when I was downstairs, so she won't come in. She and her mates are sleeping in the sitting room and watching DVDs. I would get you a toothbrush, but I don't think we have a spare. Do you want pyjamas? Because I could bring Dad's—'

'Nah, I'll get by.'

She pulled out a nightie from under the pillow, quickly stuffing it behind her back. 'Night.'

When she was gone I stripped down to my underwear, leaving my clothes in a pile on the floor, and climbed into bed.

Someone was hammering on the door.

'Ros, I want that tenner you borrowed; I'm going shopping. You can give me my top and skirt while you're at it.'

I came awake with a start.

'Don't pretend you're asleep. I know you're not.'

Disorientated, I looked around. The room was a pink blur.

'You've got five seconds. Five . . .'

Glasses. Where had I put them?

'. . . four . . . three, two, one.' The door opened as I found my specs. It was Rosalind – at least, the girl I'd thought was Rosalind, and she was absolutely gorgeous. We stared at each other a moment, me in admiration and her in shock; then the girl's face contorted.

'Who the hell are you, and what have you done with my sister?' she shrieked.

'This isn't what you think,' I said. 'I'm your sister's friend. She's sleeping in your dad's room—'

'Ros!' Olivia yelled. 'Get out here now!' To me she said, 'If you've done anything you shouldn't, I'm calling the police.'

'Promise nothing's happened—'

'I'll only believe that when my *sister* says so.'

'Everything's OK!' Rosalind appeared, wearing a faded and rather short nightie. Her eyes widened when she saw me and I self-consciously pulled the duvet up to my armpits.

Rosalind tugged at Olivia's arm. 'Livy, let him get dressed—'

'Why's he *un*dressed in the first place?'

'Slept in my underwear, that's all,' I said, fishing around on the floor for my jeans and T-shirt. 'No need to panic.'

'Who is he?' Olivia demanded. 'He doesn't go to our school.'

'He's a friend.'

'Where from?'

'The Internet.'

'You mean you don't even know the guy?'

'Yes, I do, we just haven't met face to face before.'

'Oh my God! You'd better not have done anything with him, because Dad will kill you—'

'He's not like that! Not everyone you meet on the Internet has to be a paedo or a rapist. Is it so hard to believe that I might just have made a friend?'

'OK, so he's not some pervy old man, but you're insane to invite him over. And everyone calls you the sensible one!'

'I haven't *not* been sensible. I know what I'm doing.'

'That's obvious! You planned this very carefully – sneaking him up here . . .'

'She was helping me.' I must have spoken loudly because the sisters stopped rowing and stared at me. Now I saw them together, I realized that they really did look quite alike. 'My girlfriend's gone missing. Wouldn't have got Ros involved if I thought it would get her into trouble. She's done nothing wrong.'

'He's done nothing wrong either. I can show you our online conversations if you don't believe us,' said Rosalind. 'I save them all.'

'Sad little freak,' said Olivia. 'You ought to make some real-life friends.'

'How is Jonathan not a real-life friend? He's right there.' Rosalind clenched and unclenched her hands, colour rising in her cheeks. 'You pick at everything I do!'

'Look, this isn't a big deal,' I said. 'Ros, if you're going to help me again today, we should get going soon, right?'

'Right,' said Rosalind, and gave Olivia a glare that could have killed.

'Do what you like, weirdo,' Olivia snapped. 'See if I care.'

She stomped off, no doubt to tell her mates about the strange guy she'd discovered in her sister's bed.

Rosalind shifted from foot to foot. 'That wasn't meant to happen,' she said. 'Thanks for sticking up for me.'

'Sorry if I embarrassed you.'

Rosalind sighed. Not looking at me, she went over to the wardrobe and took out a pair of dungarees. 'I'll get changed in Dad's room,' she mumbled. 'Fifteen minutes and we can go.'

Rosalind
Saturday 25 October, 10.10 a.m.

Olivia stepped into the bathroom as I was doing a quick toothbrush.

'Are you really going off with that guy?' she asked.

'He has a name,' I said. 'Jonathan.'

'Whatever. Leave your mobile on, OK?'

I swished my mouth with water. In the mirror, I saw her sigh. 'Sorry I shouted at you. Got a shock, that's all. If your friend had turned out to be an axe murderer or something, Dad would have blamed me.'

I turned, wiping my chin with a flannel. 'We really are just friends.'

'You're missing a trick there. *I* wouldn't be "just friends".'

Even when she was apologizing, Olivia couldn't resist getting in a jibe. 'See you later,' I said, pushing past.

We caught the tube. This time it wasn't busy and we sat opposite each other at the back of the last carriage.

I was wearing my retro dungarees and cap. At first I'd been hesitant, wondering if this was a step too far, then I'd reminded myself that Jonathan liked girls who dressed this way. It hadn't exactly paid off; he'd noticed what I was wearing, but only to comment, 'Freya has a hat like that' – which wasn't really what I wanted to hear.

'What's the plan?' I asked Jonathan.

'Contact the people I didn't yesterday. Only ones I'm hopeful about are Freya's neighbour back home in Norfolk and her mate Emma. Can't get through to Emma, but I know where she lives.'

'Still don't get why you don't phone her parents.'

He mimed slicing across his throat. 'Her dad's ill and he'll worry, and I bet you anything her mum will blame me. I've upset Freya enough without getting them on her back.' He sighed. 'Maybe this is all a waste of time and Freya's been caught by the *Death Line* cannibals.'

'The what?'

'*Death Line* – seventies horror film. There are these people living in the underground. They pick off lone passengers late at night and eat them.'

'That's gross!'

'When I was about ten I sneaked down to watch it after my parents had gone to bed – made me absolutely sick for days afterwards.' He paused. 'Of course, it's more likely Freya's dead in a ditch somewhere.'

'Jono, don't! Anyway, there aren't any ditches in London.'

We traded humourless smiles.

As the train entered the tunnel it struck me just how bizarre this all was. It could be a chick-flick tagline: 'Girl likes boy but keeps it hidden as she helps boy search for the girl he loves'. At first I'd felt Jonathan was making a fuss over nothing, but Freya's non-appearance at the restaurant was worrying. If she was just staying with friends, why hadn't she called work to let them know she couldn't make it? And skipping college was a bit strange too: surely she loved her music classes.

Jonathan got through to Freya's neighbour just as we arrived at Emma's.

'She's not in Norfolk either!' he exclaimed as he cut the call. 'I just hope Emma can tell us something, or I really will call the police.'

'I've been worried too,' Emma said. She was sitting on the

couch hugging a cushion to her chest, looking tired and pale. 'There are cautions in the papers about girls going out alone. Freya knows it's stupid; she even said so.'

'Where do you think she is?' asked Jonathan.

'No idea. I wish I knew.'

'We know Freya was cheating on Jonathan,' I said. 'We found some emails, and a waitress said a guy visits her at work. Know who he is?'

Emma's eyes widened. 'She never told me anything.'

'Nothing?'

'Well . . . the other day she did show off some flirty texts.' She looked at Jonathan. 'I assumed you sent them, but now I think about it, they were kind of dirty – and you don't strike me as that sort of guy.'

Jonathan opened his mouth, then closed it.

Quickly I said, 'Have you met any guys who you thought seemed keen on Freya?'

'None she liked back. If Freya does have a new guy, she's kept it very quiet. I really hope she hasn't done anything stupid. She was so upset on Saturday.'

Jonathan sighed. 'Yeah . . .'

'You were out of order shouting at her, you know.' Emma narrowed her eyes at Jonathan. 'I don't know your history, but I do know her, and she's kind and generous and totally none of the names you called her. All she wanted was a bit of space.'

★

'Well, that went well,' Jonathan said as we left.

'Maybe Emma just brings out the best in Freya, and you bring out the worst,' I said.

Jonathan shrugged. 'Weird, Emma not knowing about the new bloke. The emails Freya's been sending to Clark date back to early October, so presumably she only met him recently.'

'She could be keeping him secret because everyone knows about you and she doesn't want people to think she's a two-timer.'

He shook his head. 'Don't think that would bother her. Got to be another reason.'

'Maybe she's just enjoying having a secret?'

'Maybe. Dunno.' Jonathan looked pale. 'I'm phoning the restaurant to check she didn't turn up after we left, and then it's police time.'

'Maybe we should look some more – check out places she went a lot.'

'What good will that do? No, we've waited too long already.'

The call to the Italian drew a blank. Jonathan took a deep breath. 'You know what – I'm gonna go to Richmond. There's a police station there – I've seen it. They're the people who'll be investigating this anyway, so I may as well tell it to them. Can't exactly phone 999 for this, can I?'

I shook my head.

Jonathan
11.45 a.m.

The journey to Richmond went too quickly. Before I could blink, I found myself at the police station.

'You going in?' Rosalind asked.

I knew there was no going back now. Ros wanted to come in with me, but I made her stay outside – I didn't want her getting tangled up in this. Inside I told the policeman at reception what had happened. He asked a few questions, noted down my details and Freya's parents' number – and that was it. When I asked if there was anything I could do, I was simply told to 'get on with things as normal'.

Out on the street I met up with Rosalind. 'What now?' she asked.

I let out a long breath. 'We go home.'

Ros gave me a big hug when we said goodbye at Liverpool Street, making me promise to call with news. She'd suggested I go back to her house, but I thought it was best if I went home, especially if the police needed to contact me.

As I was finding a seat on the train my mobile rang. It was Mum.

'We need to have a serious talk, young man.' Recognizing her tone as the one she used when I was in the doghouse, I groaned. 'I've just had Moira Rose on the line. The police told them Freya's missing.'

'I know. I reported it.'

'So you were lying yesterday when you said you were round hers. I want you home right now – Moira said the police want a word, and no way am I letting that happen without your father and myself both present.'

'Will they interview me at home? I thought the London police were investigating this.'

'Don't change the subject, Jonathan. Where exactly were you yesterday?'

'OK, OK, I was staying with a mate you don't know and I thought it would be easier to say I was with Freya. We were trying to find her.'

'Who is this friend?'

'Does it matter? Just someone I met online.'

I heard Mum sigh. 'Jonathan, you know what we agreed about meeting Internet buddies. You should've at least had a friend with you—'

'I'm fine, Mum, honest. She's fourteen.'

There was silence down the line. Then Mum said, 'Did you just say *fourteen*?'

She sounded shocked; for a moment I couldn't work out why. Then I realized. 'It's not what you think,' I said quickly. 'I know it sounds a bit weird, but she was just helping me out. Nothing happened, honestly.'

'It better not have! I hope her parents were there.'

'Um, not exactly, but her big sister was. Look, Mum, you don't need to sound so horrified. She's just a friend. I didn't do anything I shouldn't have.'

Mum sighed. 'I really don't know about you any more, Jonathan! Can you promise me nothing untoward happened?'

'Yes! Of course. Anyway, do the police have any leads on Freya?'

'None that Moira mentioned. They're still getting the facts – which is why they need to talk to you as soon as possible.'

I wasn't sure I liked the sound of this. 'I'm on the train right now.'

'Good. We'll meet you at the station.'

Dad's van was waiting in the car park when I got off the train. He and Mum gave me severe looks as I climbed in beside them.

'The police have called,' Dad said. 'We've agreed to meet them straightaway.'

'Wow,' I said. 'Things are moving really quickly.'

'What did you expect?' Mum asked. 'Freya's only a child. This is serious, Jonathan.'

The officer at the desk told us to wait in the foyer and gave us a notice saying the interview would be recorded. After a little while we went through to a small room containing several chairs and a table. A man and a woman in plain clothes walked in, the woman introducing herself as Detective Inspector Shaw and her colleague as Detective Constable Turner. I looked at them as they sat, wondering if this would be like the interrogation scenes in police dramas on telly.

Shaw and Turner started by taking my parents' names and dates of birth. Then they said that they were here to advise me and ensure the interview was being conducted fairly. When Mum and Dad had confirmed for the recording that they understood, Shaw and Turner turned their attention to me.

'So, Jonathan, you're Freya's boyfriend,' said Shaw.

I cleared my throat. 'Yeah. Kind of.'

'Kind of?'

'Well, we broke up. But that's not important, right?'

They didn't answer.

'It's our understanding that Freya was last seen on Saturday night by a neighbour, leaving her aunt's house,' said Turner, 'but you were the last person to speak to her. Could you talk us through the evening?'

Going back to Saturday was the last thing I felt like doing, but I knew it was important. Letting out a long breath, I told them what had happened.

When I was done Shaw folded her arms, making me wonder if I'd said something wrong.

'So you've spoken to her friends.'

'Well, yeah. I tried ringing round yesterday.'

'You knew she was missing.'

'I suspected it yesterday lunchtime.' I glanced at the table. 'I know I should have spoken up earlier.'

'Why didn't you?'

I gave Mum and Dad a pleading look.

Mum nodded. 'The police need to know, Jonathan.'

I turned back to Shaw and Turner. 'I wanted to make sure she was missing. She'd kill me if I kicked up a fuss about nothing.'

It was the truth, but it sounded weak. I wished they'd say something, but Shaw just asked what kind of emotional state Freya was in by the time I left, and if I'd say it was out of character for her to disappear. After that there were other questions – like if she was dependent on drugs or alcohol or likely to self-harm. I wasn't sure if these were routine or whether they were trying to get at something.

'At the moment it looks as though Freya left voluntarily,' said Shaw. 'Do you have any idea where she might have been heading?'

'None. It's the walking-out-alone-at-night part that worries me. I'm scared she's been abducted.' Shaw and Turner exchanged a look, and I paused, wondering what was so significant.

'Go on,' said Shaw.

'There isn't anything else.'

'Are you sure?'

I hate it when people say that. It makes me *un*sure.

'Only thing I can think is she might have gone to see her new boyfriend, but no one knows who he is, not even her best mate.'

'New boyfriend?'

Mum and Dad looked surprised, and I felt my cheeks redden. Why hadn't I mentioned this before? Now it looked like I'd been hiding information. 'She's been cheating on me.'

'For how long?'

'Couple of weeks, I think. Really, I don't know anything.'

'Tell us what you do know.'

I wanted to lie but didn't think I could manage to convincingly. 'I looked at her email. I only wanted to see if she'd sent any messages since Saturday. She hadn't, but I found emails from some guy called "H. A. Clark".'

'How do you know Clark is male?'

'Well, I assume so, as he keeps telling her how beautiful she is.' I tried to keep the bitterness out of my voice.

'What else do these emails say?'

'More of the same – and references to meeting in the "same place", whatever that means. Oh, and he visits her at work.' I told them about my conversation with the waitress. Last night seemed a long time ago now.

Eventually Shaw and Turner appeared satisfied. 'That'll be all for the moment, Jonathan,' Shaw said. 'Thank you for coming in.'

'What happens next?' asked Dad.

'We continue the investigation. We're going through Freya's room for fingerprints, and we've a team checking CCTV footage.'

'Are you going to trace Clark?' I asked. 'You can use the IP address from his emails to find him, right?'

'You're very well-informed.'

'Jonathan's good with computers,' Mum said. 'Is there anything we can do to help?'

'Keep your phones on. We may need to talk to you again. If she turns up, we'll let you know.'

Rosalind
9.00 p.m.

When I got home, I climbed into bed, hiding under the covers. Each time I closed my eyes, I saw Freya. It didn't make sense to be upset; I didn't know or even like her – but I had, more than once, wished her out of the picture. Though I knew it wasn't possible, I couldn't help wondering if it was all my fault.

Jonathan called at about nine.

'Saw the police,' he said. 'It was a bit intimidating.'

'But they're investigating,' I said. 'That's the main thing, right?'

'Guess so. Just wish I'd reported this earlier.'

There wasn't anything much to say; Jonathan was worried sick, so were his mum and dad, so were Freya's parents, so was everyone who knew her. We filled an hour constructing theories about what might have happened until Jonathan said he had to go. I put down the phone, feeling oddly distanced from him. How much difference did it make to him that I was Rosalind, not Olivia? I'd never got a chance to ask. Our first meeting should have been about us, but without even being there, Freya had ruined it.

The first thing I did the next morning was log on to my computer. Freya's disappearance was covered on all the news sites, with most of the headlines suggesting the Student Snatcher had struck again. The reports said that police were keeping an open mind about connecting Freya to the other girls, but they admitted there were similarities. Alongside the articles was one of the photographs of Freya that Jonathan had sent me. She was posing with her cat, a big smile on her face.

There had been developments during the night. CCTV had caught Freya leaving High Street Kensington station at half ten last Saturday; at least she'd made it there in one piece. Not that that was much comfort – Kensington and Richmond were fairly close. Why Freya had gone there was another matter; High Street Kensington had good shops – I knew that from my visits to Gabe's house – but they'd have been closed by then.

The phone rang. It was Abby, bubbling with excitement.

'I saw the news. Is that the girl you were trying to find on Friday?'

'Jonathan's friend,' I said, aware I sounded bitter. 'Yeah.'

'It says she went to Kensington. Funny, isn't it? The boys might have seen her. D'you want me to text Brian and ask him?'

'Far more likely they're in league with the Student Snatcher,' I muttered – then froze. Freya wouldn't have gone to Kensington without a reason. I pictured her: emotional, upset, wanting reassurance. 'It's like Jonathan said, seek comfort in the arms of your new guy.'

'What? Which guy, Ros?'

H. A. Clark. Surely not . . . it would be a massive coincidence, but he'd said she was pretty, he'd even whistled at her. And after I'd jumped off the bus . . .

'Abby, did you see Hugh the last time you were round Gabe's?'

'Nope, he's usually off doing his own thing when we're there.'

'What's his surname – is it Clark?'

'How should I know? Ros, what's this about?'

'Got to go.' I ended the call. After the way Hugh had embarrassed me on the bus that day, it was quite possible – maybe even likely – that Freya had turned to him and asked what he meant about me stalking her. Once they were talking – well, one thing could have led to another.

Jonathan needed to know. I found his number on my phone – then stopped as the truth dawned on me.

If I told Jonathan I thought Hugh could be Freya's new boyfriend, he would want to know why. He was unlikely to believe all three of us just happened to be on the same bus. I would have to explain that I'd been following Freya – and God! My heart beat quickly. How had I *ever* thought it was OK? Stalking was strange and sick. Forget Jonathan turning out to be some dodgy old man; *I* was the one who wasn't who she seemed – I'd turned into the obsessive Internet weirdo kids were warned about. If the story ever got back to the police . . . I wasn't sure what would happen.

Worst of all, Jonathan would want to know *why* I'd followed Freya. I felt my throat constrict. I *couldn't* say why!

To hell with speaking up. I threw my phone on to the bed and tried not to think how the situation was escalating, more people getting scared and worried, just because of me.

My mobile rang. I jumped, almost falling off the chair. Lifting the cover, I saw it was Jonathan.

'Hi,' I said, trying to keep the wobble out of my voice. 'What's up?'

'It's the police.' I could hardly hear him over the voices in the background. 'They want to speak to me again. And they didn't sound happy.'

8. Idle

Jonathan
Sunday 26 October, 11.45 a.m.

I left the police station with Shaw and Turner's words ringing in my ears.

Did you hang around outside Freya's aunt's house, hoping you could see her? Did you intercept Freya when she left?

. . . Your son has a bit of a temper – and he's capable of taking it out on people who upset him. There's no doubt he was angry with Freya on the night in question . . .

. . . In our experience of missing people, it's often the last person to see them who knows more than they're letting on . . .

. . . Both these girls were abducted from the streets of south-west London, we believe by the same person. One lived a few streets from Freya. We found her body floating in the Thames . . . Where were you on the night of Saturday 27 September, Jonathan? . . .

'How dare they imply you might have had something to do with this?' Mum said as we all got in the front of the van. 'Asking for your alibi for the night that other girl disappeared, as though you were a suspect – that's ridiculous!'

'I am a suspect as far as they're concerned. I'm surprised you don't think so too.'

'Do you seriously think your dad and I believe you'd hurt

anyone? The police are clutching at straws because they're under pressure, that's all.'

'It's so unfair,' I cried. 'You mess up once and it gets held against you forever!'

It had happened last February. I never knew why Tom Copeland took against me so suddenly. He wasn't in many of my classes and we never really spoke. One day, when I was coming out of the school library, he was there with his mates. He pushed me against a wall and said I'd better watch my step. Like an idiot, I kept quiet. Two weeks later, when I'd started to relax, Tom caught me round the back of the music block after school. He must have thought I'd be easy to rough up, but he didn't know I'd been learning karate since I was little. When he laid into me, I fought back. But it wasn't like it'd been in class, sparring with someone who'd been taught the best ways to defend and block – Tom didn't know what had hit him. An adrenalin rush is a funny thing; it blows your mind. Everything's happening so fast that you can't stop.

I only realized I'd gone too far when teachers rushed in to break us up. I'll never forget the moment I set eyes on Tom. It seemed there was blood everywhere, and it was all I could do not to throw up. Someone called the emergency services; an ambulance arrived to take Tom away and the police arrived to talk to me.

I was lucky. Tom's mates swore I'd started it and if the

police had taken their word I'd have been convicted of causing actual bodily harm. As it was, someone at school must have put in a good word for me, because it was decided that there wasn't enough evidence. The police let me off with a caution, but the school suspended me until half-term.

Even now, I don't feel good about what I did. It scared me that I could hurt someone – I'd never thought I was capable of that. Tom was a bully who deserved what he got, but school wasn't the same after that and I soon ditched karate. Sometimes I had nightmares, though they'd become less frequent since starting college. I'd almost been able to kid myself it hadn't happened.

'No one's holding anything against you,' Mum said. She and Dad exchanged a look, one that said *not this again*.

'The police implied they were.'

'People can be narrow-minded,' Dad said. 'They assume the Copeland lad was the victim because he ended up in hospital.'

'The police have to bear everything in mind,' Mum added. 'Of course they'll look to see if you've anything on record; they check everyone out.'

'What if something has happened to Freya? What if they think I did it?'

'Jonathan,' Mum said softly, 'far as we know, nothing has happened. And even if it does – they can't pin anything on you. You've done nothing wrong.'

She put her arm around me. After a moment I did something I hadn't in a while; I hugged her back. I didn't believe her, but I was grateful she believed in me.

And when the police came round to the house later that afternoon, to grill me more on the Tom incident and to ask if I'd ever hit Freya, I was even more grateful. The way things were going, I was going to need all the support I could get.

Rosalind
Monday 27 October, 11.00 a.m.

It took me a long time to get to sleep on Sunday night, and when I did I had a nightmare. Jonathan and I ended up in prison, which for some reason looked like my school. He'd been done for withholding evidence and me for abduction. Our jailer was an enormous stuffed rabbit exactly like the one in Freya's room, and I kept telling it we were innocent, but it just laughed and said, 'Squee'. Then I tried to ring Abby, only I couldn't remember her number, and then I realized I was naked.

When I woke up I told myself the dream was stupid, but it wouldn't leave me, not even when I splashed my face with cold water.

Freya still hadn't been found.

The day was dragging on endlessly. At least if I had school I'd be busy, but here, all I could do was wonder if keeping quiet made me a bad person. Jonathan had phoned me again yesterday evening, sounding even more rattled than before. Apparently the police had spoken to him a third time, at his house, about that fight at school he'd had a year ago.

There was only one useful thing I could think to do. I went to Kensington.

Gabe's house looked the same as usual. I leaned against a lamp post on the other side of the road, staring ahead, hoping for some sign to tell me I was right. But no one went near a window or came out of the door.

Any normal person would have had the guts to ring the bell, but my imagination was conjuring up paranoid thoughts. Perhaps they'd fled the country, taking Freya with them. Or maybe one of them really was the Student Snatcher and they were out disposing of her body. Or perhaps she was trapped. For the first time I realized Freya wasn't some perfect person looking down on me from a pedestal. If she was in that house, she'd be as out of her depth as Abby and I were.

But then I might be wrong. Freya and Hugh could well have got off that bus without exchanging a word.

My watch showed one o'clock. I'd been here an hour.

I reasoned with myself. Nothing could happen if I

knocked on the door. They couldn't eat me. Didn't I owe it to Jonathan to do this?

I forced myself across the road and up the path to the door. The bell was still broken. Fright swelled inside me, but before I could run I'd done it, I'd knocked, and the noise seemed terribly loud.

For a few seconds it looked like no one was in. But then I heard footsteps coming down the stairs.

'Well, look who it is. Cute Ros. You really can't get enough of me, can you?'

It was Hugh. He leaned against the door frame, taking a drag on his cigarette. 'Come to take the dog out? You can if you want, seeing as he likes you so much.'

Words stuck in my throat. He leaned forward and waved a hand in front of my face.

'Hello? Planet Earth to Ros.'

It was stupid, but I hadn't been expecting him to answer and it'd thrown me. 'I . . . I came to ask a question. A couple, actually. When's your birthday – and what's your surname?'

He raised his eyebrows, and I blushed. 'Why the sudden interest? If you're planning on sending a card, you're in for a wait.'

Knowing that I must sound crazy, I decided to get to the point.

'You know that girl?'

'What girl? I know lots of girls. Have to be more specific, sweetheart.'

'The girl I was following?'

'Stalking, you mean. Go on, say it. We both know that's what you were doing.'

I felt myself blush deeper. 'OK. Fine. I was stalking her. Is she here?'

Hugh exhaled, blowing smoke at me. 'What makes you think that?'

'You liked her. You said she was pretty. You were on the bus with her.'

'You think I take every pretty girl I meet on public transport home with me? Ah, Ros, you're very sweet, but you really haven't a clue.'

'So is she here?'

He pretended to consider the question. 'Well . . . Brian and Graham and I might have her hidden in a cupboard somewhere, or chained up to the banisters, ready to do unspeakable things to. Difficult to say.' He grinned, and I backed away a few steps. 'If you really want to know . . . why don't you come in and have a look?'

I shivered.

'You're very welcome. We like it when girls come in the house. We like it even more when they don't leave . . .'

I was down the path and along the street in seconds.

Jonathan
12.00 p.m.

I hung around the house with my parents, waiting for news that never came. We didn't speak much. There was nothing to say.

Freya's parents, Moira and Owen, came over in the afternoon. Owen had always been a bit pale, but it disturbed me to see Moira looking the same. She's one of those imposing, scarily together mothers. Now everything seemed to be sapped out of her. She asked if I knew anything, over and over again. We switched on the news channel. There'd been just one development: Clark's emails had been traced to an Internet cafe in south-west London. I guessed the police had done this via the IP address; those were easy to obtain and I knew that you could enter them into databases which revealed where the email had been sent from. It looked as if Freya had been going to see Clark the night she vanished, like Ros and I thought. But loads of guys fitting the waitress's description must've used that place; the police wouldn't be able to find him with that information.

It's surreal, seeing someone you know on the news. I'd always thought of news as something that happened to other people. On one hand the report was so impersonal, but on the other it meant so much. There were a few seconds of Moira and Owen giving the usual spiel you hear from frantic parents, the kind no one listens to because it's too depressing. The newsreader can say Freya's a friendly, bubbly girl, popular with her peers and a very talented musician, but those are just words. They don't bring to life the complexities and contradictions that make Freya who she is, that make people care. The words were as useless as I felt.

The police had me in again late afternoon – the fourth time I'd seen them in three days. I sat at the table across from Shaw and Turner, wondering what they wanted this time.

'So, Jonathan,' Shaw said, 'we'd like you to talk us through what you did on those two days when you were trying to determine whether Freya was missing.'

'I've told you,' I said. 'I went to her house, checked her email, phoned a few people.'

'Where did you stay that night?'

I hesitated. 'Is this important?'

Shaw just raised an eyebrow.

'I stayed at a friend's,' I said. 'That's all.'

'And who is this friend, Jonathan?'

'Just a friend! She has nothing to do with this.'

'We think she does,' Turner said. 'She was with you when you went into Freya's house, wasn't she?'

I stared at them, feeling my heart beginning to beat more quickly. Fingerprints – I'd forgotten Ros's would have been all over Freya's stuff. There was no way I could lie my way out of this.

Slowly I said, 'If I tell you her name, will you promise not to involve her in this? All she was doing was giving me a hand – she's never even met Freya.'

The police just looked at me. Sorry Ros, I thought as I told them her name. Turner noted it down, then asked her age. I considered lying, but knew there was no point. When I said, 'Fourteen,' Shaw and Turner exchanged glances.

The next fifteen minutes were awful. The police wanted to know everything. Where had I met her? Why had I got her to help me? What had happened when I'd stayed at her house? They were particularly interested in that last question. The worst bit was when Shaw said, almost casually, 'I don't know if you're aware of this, Jonathan, but it's illegal for a sixteen-year-old to engage in a sexual relationship with a fourteen-year-old, even if it's consensual. Just something to bear in mind.'

I felt upset and humiliated – why couldn't Ros and I just be friends without everyone leaping to the wrong conclusion? Mum and Dad snapped that this questioning was out of order, but Shaw and Turner remained composed. They asked me some other questions – the same as yesterday, about the Tom incident, the missing girls, where I'd been the night Freya vanished. When I was finally allowed to go I wondered if they were going to have me in here again tomorrow, going over the same old stuff. Sooner or later I'd slip up and say something stupid – was that what they wanted?

When I called Ros that evening, I learned that the police had spoken to her too.

'It was horrible,' she said. 'They asked me all these things about you staying over and whether we'd done anything, again and again. Dad was furious.'

I felt terrible – Ros sounded so despondent. The police were really being thorough – but then I guessed they had to be. At the moment I was their only lead – and the pressure was on . . .

Rosalind
Tuesday 28 October, 9.30 a.m.

After another sleepless night I checked the news sites. Nothing had changed. I wondered if Jonathan would be called to the police station today. Though he hadn't said as much, I could tell he was dead scared, and now I knew what it felt like to be questioned I didn't blame him. It hurt so much to see him upset – especially now I felt it was my fault.

There was a knock at my door. Quickly I minimized the Internet window and tried to look normal. It was Abby.

'Men are SO rubbish,' she said, sitting on my bed. Without waiting for me to speak, she launched into her story. 'So, Claudia and I went to see Gabe and Brian. Brian said he'd made me some new jewellery so we went to his room. They were these beautiful earrings shaped like spiders' webs. We made out a little – no big deal, you know – only then he said he wanted to go all the way . . .'

'You didn't, did you?'

Abby made a huffing noise. 'I told him I wanted to think about it and he got annoyed! Said he hoped I wasn't going to be a kid about this, that he really liked me, didn't see how I could say no to having a little fun. I said we were having fun already. He told me to stop being naive and make up my mind because it wasn't fair to lead him on unless I was going to play the game. I said we should talk about it, and he got proper angry. Called me "immature"!'

'What did you do?'

'I stormed off. Went straight home.'

'You did the right thing.' I hugged her. 'You're better off without him!'

Abby shrugged. 'That was what I thought last night, but then he texted me to say sorry. He said he felt really bad about it all.'

'Don't listen to him. He's not worth it.'

She started fiddling with her bracelet. 'He wants to meet in Camden at six and take a walk by the river. Talk it all over. I said I'd go.'

'Wait a minute.' I must have sounded urgent, because she jumped a little. 'You went to the house last night? Was Hugh there?'

'Dunno, didn't see him, but he might have been in his room with someone. Brian told me Hugh's a real girl-eater. Why do you keep asking about him – d'you fancy him or something?'

'Of course not! I'm just . . .'

God, I *couldn't* keep quiet! If Hugh had hurt Freya, Jonathan would never forgive me. Yeah, the police might find her – she might turn herself in – she might mention there was a weird girl stalking her – it didn't really matter any more. This was dangerous now, and I was sick of the 'mights'.

'Are you OK, Ros?' Abby asked.

'Fine. I just need to make a phone call.'

Abby got up. 'Whatever. You've been really weird the last couple of days, Ros. Anyway, I can see this call's obviously more important than talking to me.'

She left. I barely noticed. Before I could change my mind I picked up the phone.

'Hi, Ros,' Jonathan answered in a flat-sounding voice. 'No news.'

'I have an idea where Freya is,' I blurted out. 'How soon can you be in London?'

'What? You haven't even met Freya – how could you possibly know?'

I cut the call and stood staring at the wall. My mobile rang. After a long moment I picked it up.

'You can't say stuff like that without explaining,' said Jonathan. 'Come on, Ros!'

'No. Sounds bad whichever way I put it. Can't you just trust me?'

'Can't *you* just trust me?'

'OK, OK! I think she might be at the aren't-artists' house.'

'The hell? She doesn't know them!'

'She does, kind of. See, a couple of weeks ago I was in London with one of them – Hugh. We were mucking about eating doughnuts and she passed by.' The lie came surprisingly easily. 'I only recognized her because she was wearing the same dress as in one of the photos you sent me. Hugh whistled at her. We ended up on the same bus. When I got off – well, anything might have happened between her and Hugh. Dunno what his surname is, but he fits the waitress's description.'

'Christ, Ros, why didn't you say earlier? I'd better ring the police—'

'No, please don't – I might be wrong. And even if they

did go home together, it doesn't necessarily mean anything sinister happened.'

'I'll be there soon as I can.'

Jonathan
1.05 p.m.

I got the first train I could to London. I told Mum and Dad I had a hunch that wasn't worth bothering the police with. I was astonished they let me go, but Mum just made me promise to keep my phone on, not do anything dangerous and to come home before night. I felt a rush of gratitude to my parents for trusting me, especially as I'd hardly been honest with them recently. Dad even paid my train fare. Perhaps I was luckier with my family than I realized.

Ros was waiting by the coffee stand at Liverpool Street, looking pale and drawn. She said practically nothing on the journey to High Street Kensington, despite my attempts to get her talking. We stepped out of the station on to a busy road packed with trendy shops. I started to feel intimidated. What would Hugh think when he opened the door and found a wet-behind-the-ears country boy accusing him of girlfriend stealing? His housemates might be there too and from what Ros had said I definitely didn't want to come face to face with them.

We passed an Internet cafe. A man who I guessed was the owner was standing outside smoking a cigarette, looking pissed off. If this was the place the police had traced the emails to, they'd probably have been all over it taking fingerprints and analysing CCTV footage. If Ros was right, everything I'd gone through this week could have been avoided. Why the hell hadn't she said anything earlier?

When I saw the house, I stopped.

'You really think she might be here?'

Rosalind looked nervous. 'You going to knock or shall I?'

'I can't just demand to be let in so I can look for Freya. They'll think I'm an idiot.'

'It doesn't matter what they think.'

'I know, but . . .'

'We have to do this. Come on.'

We walked up the path and she knocked. A man dressed in shirt and tie opened the door. I guessed that this was Gabe.

Rosalind glowered at him. 'We've come to see Hugh.'

'Such mature company he keeps.' Gabe headed down to the basement, leaving the door open.

'That a yes or a no?' I asked, glancing back at the road.

Rosalind stepped inside. I followed her up the stairs. As we reached the top a dog appeared and pounced on

Rosalind, tail wagging. She knelt down to scratch behind his ears, and I stepped past her into the sitting room.

I knew immediately something had happened. There was an overturned chair in the centre of the room and DVD boxes scattered across the floor, as well as a couple of broken bowls and a shattered glass ashtray. I guessed they'd been sitting on the small cabinet by the TV, which was now lying on its side, one of its legs snapped. The couch was at a funny angle, the cushions all over the place, and the mat in the centre of the room was creased and crumpled.

'Ros,' I called, 'come and have a look at this.'

She came in, the dog at her heels. Her eyes widened when she saw the mess. After a pause, she said, 'It might have been Gabe's friends. Hugh told me they smashed the place up once.'

If Freya was here, I hoped she'd kept well out of the way. I was about to go upstairs when I spotted patterned fabric peeping out from under a cushion. I pulled it out – and felt my stomach turn.

'Jono?' Ros was at my side. 'What's up?'

Her eyes fastened on the distinctive reddish stain in the fabric.

'Blood,' I said, hearing my voice wobble. 'Ros, this is one of Freya's scarves.'

'You sure?'

'Positive, it's one of her favourites. Christ, what if we're too late?' I was trembling all over.

'*Shit!*' said Ros.

I could see a couple of small stains on the floorboards now and horrible images of Freya being beaten up were shooting through my head. 'If she's still here, we need to find her – quickly!'

The stairs creaked as we climbed up, increasing my sense of foreboding. Five doors led off the landing at the top, two on one side, two on the other, one facing us, all closed. There was also another staircase immediately to our left. If anyone was in the rooms, they weren't making any noise. I looked at Ros. She frowned.

'That one at the end is Brian's room. I don't know about the others though.'

I knocked frantically on the nearest door on the right. No answer. After a moment I opened it – but there was nothing inside apart from boxes and other junk.

'Jono!' Ros was standing by the next door along with the dog. 'I've found Hugh's room – there are some envelopes with his name on and he is H. A. Clark – but there's something else . . .'

I joined her and followed her gaze to sheets of photos, spread out across the desk. For a moment I was dumbfounded. Although the photos were obviously Freya – at the same time, they weren't. While some were just pretty head shots, a couple were more risqué – in one, all she appeared to be wearing was some kind of sheet. Freya had always been scathing about this kind of photography – evidently Hugh had changed her mind. What the hell had been going on?

Sick to my stomach, I pushed past Ros and flung open the door opposite Hugh's – but the room was empty.

'The last one's just a bathroom,' Ros said. 'I don't think she's here, Jono.'

'What about up there?' I nodded to the staircase.

'I don't think they use those rooms; Gabe said the house was too big . . .' Ros trailed off. She was staring at the steps, and I realized what she was thinking: a staircase no one used wouldn't have had footprints showing in the dust.

'Bloody hell,' I said in a low voice as we made our way up. 'God, Ros, what if she's dead?'

Ros just gave me a panicked look. At the top of the staircase was a landing with the same layout as below. The trail of dusty footsteps led to the nearest door. I took a moment to steel myself for what might be inside – and opened it.

This was a cross between a storage room and a bedroom: crates stacked against one wall, manky-looking unmade camp bed against the other. No dead bodies. Suddenly realizing how shaky my legs were, I sat down heavily on the bed.

The dog started sniffing around. Something had caught his interest and he wriggled under the bed. Ros crouched down to look. 'Apples,' she said, reaching and taking the packet from the dog. 'Just one left now – rotten. Well, that explains the smell in here.'

'Whoever was here hasn't been here since the end of August,' I said, reading the sell-by date.

'There's something else,' Ros said. She pulled out a necklace. It was a purple gem set in silver, with elaborate patterns round the edge. The black cord it was attached to had been snapped. I took it, turning it over in my hand. It wasn't Freya's style, but something about that necklace was familiar . . . where had I seen it before?

Snapping back to the present I got up, dropping the necklace on the bed. 'Let's get out of here.'

Ros nodded, picking up the necklace and stuffing it in her pocket. Quickly we went downstairs, hurrying through the living room and to the front door, desperate to get away. The dog tried to follow us out, but I forced him back in. Outside we careered into an elderly lady who was dumping a black sack into a wheelie bin. She scowled at us.

'More running around!'

'Sorry,' I said. 'Wait – what do you mean?'

'Last night's what I'm talking about! One of these days I'm making a complaint about your friends in that house. Worst neighbours I've ever had!'

'What happened last night?'

The woman made a huffing noise. 'There was some kind

of argument – lots of shouting and crashing about. I looked out the window to see what was going on and saw one of them storming out. Someone was yelling at him from inside, kept saying something about "your girlfriend poking about" and "warning you to keep your mouth shut". I didn't like his tone at all!'

'Which one of them left?' I asked urgently. 'Was there a girl with him?'

'It was the scruffy one who fancies himself as a photographer.' She wrinkled her nose. 'As for the girl, she left too, all dolled up like something out of the sixties.'

Freya! Heavy with relief, Ros and I headed back to the high street.

'We'd better tell the police about this, Jono,' Ros said in a small voice. 'Let them know she's safe.'

I opened my mouth to reply – and then it hit me. Suddenly I knew where I'd seen that necklace before. Spying a newsagent, I rushed in and grabbed a newspaper. As I'd hoped, there was a Student Snatcher report. By the text was the photo the press had been using of Lyndsey, the second missing girl – and, sure enough, round her neck hung a purple gem.

Ros's eyes widened.

Rosalind
2.00 p.m.

'Oh, Christ!' Jonathan swallowed. 'Freya left with him, *alone*. She's not safe at all!'

The newsagent was looking at us curiously. I pulled Jonathan outside. My heart was beating so quickly I was sure he could hear it. I felt terrible; I'd sort of liked Hugh. The thought that he'd taken Freya to his house – and Lyndsey before her – *killed* that first girl – it was too much to get my head round –

'Wait a moment,' I said. 'This doesn't follow.'

'What?'

'That neighbour said something about "girlfriend poking about".'

'So?'

'So, it sounds as if Hugh and Freya were being threatened by someone else. Maybe Freya found something she wasn't supposed to.'

Jonathan snapped his fingers. 'The room upstairs! Those footprints looked pretty fresh to me.'

'That could be why there was a fight! And why they left!'

'But wait. If Hugh's not the killer, then who is?' Jonathan asked.

I grimaced, thinking back to the first time I'd met the aren't-artists and, even then, how creepy I'd found Gabe . . .

I mentioned it to Jonathan. He looked appalled. 'That guy who opened the door to us? That's mental, Ros!'

'I didn't say it *was* him! Maybe. I don't know what to think any more! All I know is he and his house freak me out. Why *did* he invite me, Abby and Claudia round?' The full impact of this hit me as I spoke. We'd been casually hanging out in the home of a man who might be a *murderer* –

'Maybe he was looking for his next victim?'

'Let's not go there! Jono, this is way too big for us. Whatever's happened, whether it's Hugh or Gabe involved, something is seriously wrong. We've got to phone the police!'

'Ros, no!' Jonathan cried, the sharpness in his voice making me jump. 'We can't! Christ, don't you realize? My prints are all over that necklace – *and* the house – and this!' He waved the bloodied scarf. 'I'm already a suspect – now the police are *really* going to think I did it!'

I looked away, feeling helpless, horrified and sick all at once. 'So what do we do?'

'I don't know!'

A woman walking past gave us a funny look.

'Only one thing for it,' Jonathan said in a calmer voice. 'We've got to find Freya. We find her, make sure she's safe. Then we're off the hook – the police's suspicions about me won't hold up and we'll be free to tell them what we've found at the house. So –' he took a breath – 'any idea where she might be?'

I stared at him. 'How am I supposed to know, Jono?'

'Well, Hugh must've taken her somewhere. And you know more about Hugh than I do.'

'Not much!'

It was beginning to feel like we were trapped in a horror film, the kind where the gruesome shocks keep coming even when you think there can't possibly be any more. 'I hardly know Hugh well enough to know where he'd have taken Freya.'

'They left yesterday, so they've stayed somewhere overnight. Maybe they went to some friends of Hugh's? Family? A hotel?'

'He never mentioned—' I stopped.

Hugh's photos. A picture of a boat – his dad's. I remembered it because it seemed so strange – houseboats in London. Would he have taken Freya there?

'It's possible,' Jonathan said when I told him. 'Any other ideas?'

I shook my head. Everything inside me was screaming that trying to play detective was a bad, even dangerous, idea. I wanted to run away, go home and hide in my bed and pretend this mess didn't exist. For all I knew, we were heading for another dead end.

Jonathan
3.05pm

We had to waste time finding an Internet cafe because Ros didn't know where the houseboats were moored – 'Little Venice' could have been anywhere. A quick Google told us that we needed to head to Maida Vale, not far from where we were now. An underground journey and a short walk and we were there. As I took in the colourful boats moored at the banks and the backs of the tall, straight houses bordering the water I began to realize this wouldn't be easy.

'What's the boat called?' I asked Ros.

'Dunno. A girl's name, I think. And there were mermaids painted on it.'

Not much to go on, I thought. Quite a few of the boats seemed to have female names. And the canal was long – Ros and I had looked it up in her little London *A–Z*. We didn't know Hugh's dad's first name either, so asking people was pointless. The passers-by all looked like tourists anyway.

After an hour, I began to feel frantic.

'It's like searching for a needle in a haystack,' I said. 'How can we find something when you don't even know if you'll recognize it?'

Ros was frowning at a greyhound wandering along the path a few feet away. Without a word she went over and started to stroke him. The dog wagged its tail.

'Are you even listening?' I asked crossly. 'Christ, Ros, what is it with you and dogs?'

'Lovely, isn't he?' a woman on the boat nearest to us called. 'Rudi's quite an old boy now, bless him, but he's always got a hello for visitors.'

'Is he yours?' Ros asked.

'Nope, he's Russell's, though he visits me now and again, especially if I'm baking cakes.'

'Which one's Russell's boat?'

'That green and red one just up there.'

Ros looked over her shoulder at me. 'Come on. I think Russell must be Hugh's dad.'

'What?'

'There was a dog in the photo of the boat Hugh showed me – this dog, I think.'

Quickly we went up to the boat the woman had indicated. I felt my heart begin to pound. The boat's nameplate read *Annabel*. Rudi swaggered on board like he owned the place and disappeared inside.

'That's it – Annabel!' Ros cried. 'It's been repainted since the photo was taken. No wonder we couldn't find it.'

A bearded man was sitting on the deck frowning at an easel. Without looking up, he said, 'D'you mind moving? You're in my light.'

'Oh. Sorry.' My throat felt suddenly dry. 'Um, is Hugh about?'

'Hugh!' the man yelled. I wiped sweaty palms on my jeans, hoping against hope that Freya was all right.

A guy emerged from the boat. He fitted the waitress's description, though right now the area around his nose looked bruised and uncomfortable. Seeing us, he raised his eyebrows.

'I'm starting to seriously wonder about you, Ros. What are you doing here? Come to show off your boyfriend or something?'

'I'm not her boyfriend,' I said.

There was a thump from within. A familiar, tousled head appeared behind Hugh's shoulder.

'God,' said Freya. 'Jonathan.'

I stared, almost unable to believe my eyes. Then, in sheer relief, I stepped on deck and pulled her into a hug. She tensed at first, but then brought up a hand and patted my shoulder.

'OK, Jonny, back off. Why are you here?'

I let her go, opening my mouth to say how relieved I was. Then reality smacked me in the face. Freya was with another bloke. From the looks of things, she was wearing one of his shirts. All the police interviews, the worry, the stress I'd been under – and here she was acting like nothing had happened!

'Why do you think I'm here?' I exclaimed. 'You've been gone for over a week! No one had a clue where you were.'

She folded her arms. 'I'm totally within my rights to

go away if I want to.'

'Freya, come on! Didn't it occur to you that people would wonder where you were?'

'I didn't want people bothering me – especially not you, Jonathan! How did you even find me?'

'I know that one,' said Hugh. 'It's cos Ros here is your devoted stalker. Isn't that right, sweetheart?'

Behind me Rosalind coughed nervously.

I ignored Hugh, keeping my attention on Freya. 'I was worried sick something had happened to you.'

'Well, it hasn't – though things got nasty last night with Hugh's housemate.'

'What? With Gabe?'

Hugh snorted. 'No, he's been as nice as pie all week. Brian's the one who went psycho when Freya had a look round the attic. He's a nutter!'

Brian? I glanced at Ros. She was looking baffled.

'What happened?' I asked.

Freya shrugged. 'I was only looking for interesting props. We were doing a photo shoot. Hugh said there were loads of boxes on the top floor with stuff that belonged to Gabe's auntie. One of the rooms had been made into a bedroom. Later on I was joking to Hugh about how people could be living up there without anyone knowing. Brian overheard me, and for some reason he just lost it!'

'He didn't hurt you, did he?'

'I think he might have, if Hugh hadn't been there.'

'Yeah, and Hugh's nose is regretting being there.' Hugh winced, and then I realized. The blood on the scarf wasn't Freya's at all. It was Hugh's!

'Poor Hughie,' Freya was saying. 'We'd been having such a fun week.'

Fun! For an instant, I was speechless. Then I was furious.

'I suppose you were having so much fun that you decided to skip your classes and your work shift and became totally oblivious to the outside world. What the *hell* do you think you're playing at? You've been reported missing! Your picture's all over the news, for Christ's sake!'

'Oh, tell me that's a joke!' Freya's face dropped. 'You idiot, Jonathan!'

I wasn't standing for that and I didn't give a damn if I was shouting. 'Don't you dare call me an idiot. Two girls from south London went missing. One was murdered! Did the thought not pop into your empty head that people might think you were dead too? Or that the police might think I did it? I've been questioned four times!'

For a moment she looked stupefied. Then she put on a haughty face. 'I can take care of myself!'

'Yeah, I'm sure that's what the first girl thought too! Don't give me that shit.' She tried to speak, but I didn't let her. 'I've had it with telling you how bloody selfish you've been. You'd better let the police know you're all right, cos they're this close to arresting me, and your parents are frantic with worry!' I looked at Ros. 'Come on. Let's go.'

Ignoring Freya calling after me, I left, and I was glad I had my back to her, because this way she couldn't see how near to crying I was.

Rosalind
5.30 p.m.

'Jonathan,' I called, sprinting to catch up with him. He was walking very quickly, looking straight ahead.

'God, I never realized how thoughtless she can be. I am so over this shit! How did she think that people wouldn't worry?'

'Dunno.' I was a little breathless and the words come out huskily. 'But look, Jono, what do you think about what Hugh said about Brian? It doesn't fit, does it? Gabe's the creepy one –'

Jonathan frowned at me as though the answer was obvious. 'Well, we were wrong. Brian's the Student Snatcher – it's obvious.'

As soon as he said it, everything came together. I remembered how weird Brian had been when Abby and I had left the house. How insistent he'd been that Abby stay. I thought of the missing girls. Now I came to think of it, they both looked a bit gothy, like Abby . . . Abby, who was due to meet Brian at Camden in half an hour! Suddenly realizing what this could mean – and angry at how slow I'd been on the uptake – I grabbed Jonathan's arm.

'Abby's in trouble!'

I explained.

Jonathan looked alarmed. 'Do you think he'd hurt her?'

'Maybe! I don't know!'

'OK, let's not get carried away. Give Abby a ring.'

I pulled out my phone. Abby's number went straight to voicemail.

'She must be on the tube already.' I felt my stomach sink. 'It goes into the tunnel at East Finchley – that means she's twenty minutes from Camden Town station, max. It's five thirty now – she was due to meet him at six – she's early!'

'Where were they meeting?'

'I don't know!'

'Ros, chill. If you keep ringing, you can get through the moment she comes out.'

'But what if she doesn't pick up? Maybe they're meeting right outside the station. I won't be able to catch her before he does!' Something else hitting me, I cried, 'She said they were going to go for a walk by the *river*! Jono, the dead girl's body was found in the Thames!'

We stared at each other.

Jonathan swore. 'How far is Camden?'

I wiped my eyes, angry that I was losing it like this. 'Ages away! Three different tube lines!'

As we stood trying not to panic Hugh and Freya passed us – presumably on their way to the police station.

Hugh raised his eyebrows at me. 'You OK?'

'No!' Against my better judgement, I poured everything out. For the first time since I'd met him, Hugh looked perplexed.

'Seriously, Ros, is this some kind of joke? I live with the guy. I think I'd know if murdering teenagers was one of his hobbies!'

'Why did he get so mad at Freya for finding the room then?'

Hugh was shaking his head, but he wasn't looking sure of himself. 'This is flipping insane.'

'And how do you explain the necklace?' I continued, almost in tears. Whether it was this or what I'd said, something seemed to click into place for Hugh.

'OK, Ros. Don't stress! I know exactly where Brian is. It's Tuesday – he'll be at his stall at Stables Market.'

He looked at Freya. 'Go!' she cried. 'I'll go to the police station – and call them on my way!'

'Right!' Hugh said. 'Let's get moving!'

'But we can't get over there in time!' I said. 'It's impossible.'

'Ah, Ros. Such a pessimist.' Hugh took some notes out of his pocket and waved them at me. 'Raided Dad's wallet. Taxi, anyone?'

We were at Maida Vale station in a few minutes. Some tourists were just getting out of a cab and we hailed it, Hugh shouting to Freya that he'd join her as soon as he could.

'Should only take ten minutes or so to get there,' Hugh said when we were on the move. 'Can't quite get my head around all of this, but in a way it fits . . .'

'What makes you say that?' I asked.

Hugh made a face. 'Well, he was the one who made the meeting with you, Abby and Claudia happen.'

'Huh? I thought it was Gabe who wanted to meet us.'

'Nope. Gabe brought Claudia home one night and she was showing us pictures on her phone, and once Brian saw one of Abby he kept going on about how we should all meet up. He's always been a bit full-on when it comes to girls – took his last break-up really badly.'

We sat in silence for the rest of the way, trying to digest this uncomfortable information. In just under fifteen minutes we were outside Stables Market. I'd tried Abby's phone continuously. The last call had started ringing – which meant she wasn't underground any more. But she hadn't picked up.

There was no sign of the police as we entered the market's

main yard – but then it hadn't been long ago that Freya had called. Colourful stalls and shops, mostly selling clothing, accessories and fast food, were set back from the cobbled walkways in recesses. Some of them were playing pounding music, which seemed at odds with the fancy metal benches and statues of horses in the main area.

'Do you know where Brian's stall is?' I asked. Hugh nodded. Hoping we'd arrived ahead of Abby, I took the nearest walkway. It looked like the market was winding down for the day, meaning that we couldn't conceal ourselves in the crowd. Not that Brian was going to do anything to us if we were spotted . . . at least, I hoped not.

'We have a problem,' Hugh said suddenly. I followed his gaze to an empty shop some metres ahead. 'That's where Brian usually is. He must've packed up early!'

Maybe this wasn't where they were meeting after all! Panic rising, I looked around, hoping vainly to see Abby or Brian in the crowd, or some kind of clue to tell me where they were. Nothing – and then I caught sight of Brian, heading up the walkway carrying an empty crate. It was impossible to read anything from his expression – he just looked mildly bored. And normal. I began to wonder if we'd been barking up the wrong tree. He reached his shop and perched on the table, checking his watch. We backed behind a stall so he couldn't see us.

'Must've been taking everything to the car,' Hugh

whispered. 'Main thing is, your mate's not here yet.'

Feeling heavy with relief, I tried Abby's phone again. Still no answer.

'We can get to her before she even reaches him,' Jonathan said. 'If you think about it – she could come from three different directions. Let's split up – and you keep ringing, Ros.'

'The boy talks sense,' Hugh said. Jonathan scowled at him. He walked past Brian's stand and I drew in breath sharply – then remembered that Brian and Jonathan had never met. I retreated a few steps, ducking behind a rail of coats. Hugh slipped down a nearby alley.

Brian finished clearing the stand. He leaned against the glass front. He'll be on the lookout now, I thought – and then Abby appeared round the corner at the far end of the walkway. Jonathan stepped into her path. Abby looked startled, glancing over at Brian's stall. Jonathan put his hand on her arm and they hurried back the way Abby had come. But Brian was also moving – in their direction. The intense look that had suddenly come on to his face made my blood run cold.

'This way,' Hugh hissed from the alleyway. I followed him and came out on to the next parade. Jonathan and Abby appeared at the far end and headed out of the back exit. Brian followed them, just a few seconds behind. Hugh and I hastened to the gate, dodging stalls and tourists. Please don't let him catch them, I thought as we pushed our way out. Jonathan and Abby were running up the street, but they kept having to swerve out of the way of passers-by. Brian was doing the same, but I could see he was closing on them. I opened my mouth to yell this to Hugh – then two police cars swerved round the corner, sirens blazing.

Jonathan, Abby and I stood outside Abby's house. The police had taken Brian off for questioning and Hugh had gone with them. They said they'd be talking to us later, which was good, as I wasn't sure if Abby was in a fit state for answering questions. Once everything had been explained she'd started to shake uncontrollably. The whole journey home she'd kept repeating, 'It can't be him. He's a nice person.'

The police officer who'd given us a lift back was in the house explaining the situation to Abby's parents. Telling Abby I'd follow her inside in just a moment, I looked at Jonathan.

'I guess you'll be going now.'

'I'd better. I promised Mum and Dad. They're not going to believe all this!' He turned, then paused. 'Ros . . . why didn't you say anything earlier about where Freya was? And what did Hugh mean by "devoted stalker"?'

My stomach twisted. 'I didn't do anything wrong, really. I never meant any harm.'

'What – you really did stalk Freya?'

'No, I . . . Let me explain.' There was no way out now and I was almost glad I could tell the truth at last. 'You went on and on about Freya, but I couldn't understand what made you like her so much. I wanted to see for myself – I was curious.'

Jonathan frowned. 'OK – that's creepy. Like, really creepy.'

'I know! That's why I didn't say anything – didn't want anyone to know. And . . . there's something else I wanted to keep secret.' I wet my lips. 'Something that might make more sense.'

I squeezed his arm, mostly because I was afraid of losing my nerve. I thought for a moment about how to put my feelings into words and then decided that maybe it didn't matter. Taking a deep breath, I managed to smile.

'I really like you. Love you, maybe.'

He stared at me. My smile wavered.

'I thought that if I knew what you liked about her, then maybe I could work out how to make you like me.' His expression was unnerving me now. 'Say something.'

Jonathan shook his arm from mine, staring at me as though I was a lunatic.

'You're far too young for me! You're fourteen, Ros!'

I opened my mouth to tell him I might be only a kid, but that didn't change what I'd done for him. I'd been there the times he wanted to talk, I'd bunked off school when he needed me and I'd sat up into the early hours comforting him. My age didn't change what we'd shared and the jokes we'd made or anything at all, if what we had was as strong as I'd thought it was.

I could have said all these things, but I didn't. Instead, I just went inside.

9. Offline

Rosalind
8.00 p.m.

In an odd way I was almost glad that the last few hours had been like an episode of *Crimewatch*, because it meant I didn't have to think about Jonathan. Abby's parents had lots of questions to ask and it was ages before we could escape to her room and be alone. The police had returned to tell us that Brian had confessed under questioning to the murder of the first girl. I'd suspected that hours ago, but to hear it confirmed really rammed everything home.

After a while Abby said quietly, 'Brian always scared me a little. But I never admitted it because I was jealous of you.'

'Me? Why?'

'You had Jonathan. He was so much cooler than any of the boys that ever liked me.'

I sighed. 'Jealousy does funny things to people.'

'Why do you think Brian did what he did?'

'I don't know. Hugh seemed to think it all started when he got dumped a while back.'

Abby made a small noise and I put my arm around her. We were silent for a while. Then Abby said, 'If it wasn't for you, I might be dead right now.'

'We don't know that's what he was planning,' I said quickly.

'I sort of dumped him too though, didn't I? When he wanted to . . . you know, I said no. Maybe he wanted to make me pay. And then when I was dead . . .' She shivered. 'He'd just move on to someone else.'

Perhaps that was the pattern. Brian targeted girls he thought he'd be happy with, then flipped when they rejected him. There had been a man on the news like that; every time he'd started off with the best intentions, believing that this girl would be different from the last.

'I was dating a cold-blooded murderer!' Abby said. 'This is the kind of thing that happens in films, Ros! Not to people like us.'

'It did though,' I said, squeezing her hand. 'But, Abby? I'm so glad you're OK.'

The next day the Student Snatcher was front-page news in all the papers and websites – partly because Freya was safe, but also because the second girl, Lyndsey, had walked into a police station last night and told her story. Apparently she'd met Brian in a goth club. She'd been unhappy at home, and after a couple of weeks Brian had invited her to stay round his house in the attic room. Everything had gone well for a while, but then Brian and Lyndsey had had an argument that had led to blows, and Lyndsey had managed to get out of the house. Terrified by his threats, she'd been lying low, staying with some friends who lived far away and keeping quiet about the whole thing. I did the maths and worked out that a couple of days after Lyndsey had left was when Brian had first met Abby, which I guessed fitted the pattern.

The news reports didn't say much else, though one had published an interview with Gabe. 'I am completely shocked by what's happened,' he was quoted as saying. 'If I'd known my housemate was picking up young girls and taking them to my house, I'd have asked him to leave.'

Under other circumstances that would almost be funny.

On the last day of half-term the doorbell rang. Knowing I was the only one home, I opened the door.

It was Hugh – with Dog.

'*Bonjour, Mademoiselle.*'

I wasn't sure what to say. This was the last thing I expected. Hugh looked different – smarter – and he'd actually had a shave. 'How do you know where I live?'

'I have amazing powers of detection! No, really, I got your mate Claudia to tell me.'

'She's not my mate,' I snapped, and Hugh grinned.

'Still uppity, I see.'

'Oh, shut up,' I said, and immediately wondered how I had the nerve. 'What do you want?'

'Came to give you an early Christmas present.' He held out Dog's lead, which appeared to be made of several ties knotted together. 'Yours if you want him.'

I stared. 'You serious?'

'The police are all over the house and it's doing my head in; I'm off for a couple of weeks. Graham won't look after him. I seem to recall you saying you'd always wanted a dog.'

'I have, but Dad would never let me.'

'Play the poor neglected child traumatized by divorce and I bet he will.'

I looked at him sharply. 'How do you know . . .'

He shrugged. 'I can tell. And trust me, it works.'

I found myself taking the lead. 'Thanks, I guess.'

'No need for thanks – it's no skin off my nose.'

'Good. Your nose needs all the skin it can get.'

Hugh looked startled, then he laughed. 'Nice one, Ros!' I hid a smile. 'See you around, OK?'

He stepped out on to the pavement and it was then that I saw Freya waiting. She looked at me a moment, then linked arms with Hugh. He gave me another wave and they headed off.

Something butted my leg. Dog was looking up at me.

I smiled. 'You look ridiculous. Didn't they even buy you a proper lead and collar? Let's get these undone and I'll get you something to eat.'

'Christ, Ros!' Olivia stepped through the open door.

'Where did the dog come from?'

I thought a moment. 'I guess a friend gave him to me.'

'Are you planning on keeping him? Dad isn't going to like it one bit.'

'He'll have to get used to it,' I said with a shrug. 'Now, are you going to help me figure out how I explain this or not?'

Olivia entered my room without knocking. I looked up from where I was sitting on the bed with a freshly bathed Dog beside me, sketchpad on my knees.

'I cannot believe you talked Dad round.'

I shrugged. 'Just played the poor neglected child traumatized by divorce.'

'All right, what happened? All you've done the last few days is sit up here drawing.'

I thought about the sketches I'd done. Jonathan, Freya, Hugh, the police – everything I'd gone through in the last week had tumbled out on to the paper. I wasn't sure if drawing them made me feel better or worse, but it seemed the right thing to do. What I was sure about was that I'd never show these pictures to anyone.

I shrugged.

Olivia sat down beside me. 'Come on, Ros. Is it anything I can help with?'

I nearly laughed. I couldn't remember Olivia ever

offering me help. She was persistent though, and finally got the whole story out of me. I'd expected her to be scathing, but she just shook her head.

'God, Ros, you need to get out more. You could have been in big trouble, you know that? And seriously, were you expecting the guy to say, "Sure, be my girlfriend"?'

'He could have told me he liked me but didn't want to go out with anyone now – or something! It hurts!'

'Well, yeah. If it doesn't hurt then it never meant anything.'

'It's all right for you. You've got your mates and your boyfriend. I never really had anyone apart from Abby until Jonathan started chatting to me.'

'You had me.'

I glared at her. 'You never have time for me any more – far too busy! We don't even talk about Mum now. It's like she never mattered.'

'Don't you dare say that!'

'It's true, isn't it?'

'No, it's total crap! You hide what you feel all the time, Ros, and yet you don't seem to understand that other people do too. I started my period a month after Mum walked out. To most people that's a mother–daughter event. But I had to go out and buy sanitary towels myself and I didn't even have my mates' help because I was the first. At least you've had me to explain things like that.'

Feeling a bit guilty, I mumbled, 'I never knew.'

'Of course Mum meant something to me. Don't be thick.'

I shrugged, glancing up at the ceiling. The Great Britain-shaped stain was still there – I wondered if Dad ever would get round to painting over it. 'It's not much fun round here any more.'

'I know. And I think you've been bottling your feelings up too much,' she said softly.

'I told Jonathan how I felt. He was good at making me see things for what they were.'

'You can talk to me. I'm not always here, but that doesn't mean I don't have time for you.'

I glanced up at her, trying to remember if Olivia had ever been this gentle before.

She gave me a half-smile. 'I do love you, you know.'

'Yeah. And I love you. I know you don't mean it when you call me a weirdo.'

'Well, most of the time,' she said, and that made both of us laugh.

When Olivia left, I logged on to MyPlace and deleted Jonathan from my contacts list.

Jonathan
Tuesday 28 October, 8.00 p.m.

On the train home I sat with my feet on the seat and my knees up to my chest and leaned my head against the window. Things were taking a while to sink in. My mind should be on Freya – or the fact that I'd helped stop a cold-blooded murderer in his tracks – but instead I found myself thinking about Ros.

I had every right to be furious with her. She'd stalked my girlfriend, told me a bunch of lies and withheld information from the police when she knew how worried everyone was. And she did it because she 'loved' me. Call me naive, but I'd never really thought there was an ulterior motive behind her helping me out – it just felt natural. Now I knew why she'd bunked off school and sat up into the early hours chatting. I'd never meant to give her ideas – but I guessed she couldn't help how she felt. After all, I knew what it was like to love someone who didn't feel the same way.

It made sense. But whether I felt like forgiving Ros or not, I wasn't sure.

Mum and Dad picked me up from the station. They looked tired but they smiled as I got in the van and said how glad they were to see me safe. Back home, after a big bowl of pasta, we sat in front of the fire and they asked me to explain how I knew where Freya was. There was no way to do this quickly so I told them everything – almost everything, anyway. When I was done, Dad shook his head.

'Beggars belief, all of this. Anyone want tea?'

I watched him go through to the kitchen. 'I got wound up in a murder inquiry and that's all he's going to say?'

'You know the way your father's mind works,' Mum said. 'All of these to-and-fros from London have probably lost him.' She paused. 'So . . . your friend Rosalind. Any idea why she followed Freya about London? That's the only part that doesn't make sense to me. Unless . . .'

The gleam in her eye was back.

I went red. 'Shut up, Mum.'

I half-expected her to say something about Ros's age, but she did as I said. Deciding to change the subject quickly, I crossed the room and sat beside her on the couch. 'Mum . . .'

'Yes?'

'Sorry I've been a pain. I've mucked you and Dad about lately, and some of the time it wasn't fair.'

'I'm glad you realize that. Just let us know where you are and who you're with in future, all right?'

I nodded. 'And Mum . . .' I took a breath. 'About the music. I – I'm sorry I got so angry with you and Dad about it . . . but you didn't seem to understand how important it is to me. I might not be the best, but it's what I want.'

Mum nodded. She didn't seem surprised. 'Jonathan . . .

your Dad and I have been talking. I think we owe you an apology too. You're right – we did push you a bit, but we never wanted you to be unhappy. So we've come up with an idea. Is it too late for you to change your subjects?'

I blinked. This I hadn't expected. 'What, drop something and take music instead?'

She nodded. 'You could switch further maths for music. If it's not too late, that is.'

'Don't think so. I mean, we're only half a term into the academic year.'

'I know an A level isn't quite music school, but it keeps music open if you decide that's where you want to be after college.'

'You'd really support me in this?'

'Jonathan, these are your A levels, not ours. I want you to be happy at college – and if music will make you happy, you have to do it.' She smiled. 'And you know, your dad and I will always back you, whatever you decide to do'

I felt elated. What a mess this whole thing had been – but if this had come out of it . . . 'I'll talk to my tutor after half-term. Thanks, Mum.'

Moira and Owen came over the next day. I thought they'd just come to say thank you when Mum called me down, but Freya was with them.

'Freya has something she wants to say,' Moira said, giving

Freya the sternest look ever – clearly relief at having her daughter safe had worn off already. Freya shifted on her feet. For the first time I could remember, she looked awkward.

'Sorry,' she mumbled. 'I never meant to make anyone worry.'

'She's promised to think more in future, so nothing like this will ever happen again,' Moira said briskly, and then started talking to Mum and Dad.

Freya looked at me. 'Can I have a word, Jonny?'

We went through into the next room, closing the door behind us. It was almost like old times, the two of us, here in my house, and for a moment I allowed myself to fantasize that she was about to take me back.

'What?' I asked, suddenly realizing I didn't want that.

Freya circled her foot on the floor, not looking at me. 'I feel awful about you getting into trouble with the police.'

I shrugged.

'Jonny, I know you're mad at me and I probably deserve it, but I never meant for this to get so messy. You'll call me stupid, and maybe I am, but I didn't realize people would go searching for me. I don't know if you'll understand, but while I was with Hugh I just stopped thinking straight.'

I did understand. Sometimes you meet someone so blinding, so enticing, that you lose all judgement and reason. For Freya, that's Hugh. For me, it was Freya. And I guess for Ros, it's me.

'And I'm sorry I broke up with you in such a bad way. I hope you're not going to hate me forever.' Freya was looking at me like a little girl who'd been caught stealing chocolate.

I knew what she wanted, but she wasn't getting it. For once I was calling the shots. 'You've apologized; you prefer a penniless photographer over an aspiring rock star, fine, great. Now, is there anything else you need to say? I'm actually really busy today.'

'You're different.' She frowned at me, tipping her head. A strand of hair fell out of its clip and on to her shoulder. For a moment I felt a pang, remembering the early days, when Freya and her crazy hair were the most fascinating things in the world. 'Don't know how, but you are.'

'Well, thanks for the almost profound observation, Freya. See you round, OK?'

In my room I picked up my guitar and started to strum, thinking about Freya. I guessed a little part of me was still in love with her, but mostly I was relieved I knew where I was, even if it hurt – actually, that might make a good story for a song, if I could get some words down to go with the melody I'd just started to pick out. I grabbed my notebook. Two hours later I had three verses and a chorus and I was excited, yes, excited about music again. I'd thought I couldn't write without Freya, but I'd been wrong. The inspiration and the words were in me – it had just taken a long time to realize it.

*

On Monday students mobbed me on the zombie bus. Everyone had heard about Freya and the case and wanted to know all the details. I wasn't sure I liked being the centre of attention, so at lunchtime I hid in the computer labs. But I wasn't alone for long – Lucy came in. I sighed.

'Look, Lucy . . .'

'If you want to get away from all the questions, a bunch of us are playing card games in Room 4.' She didn't look at me as she said this. 'Welcome to join us if you want to.'

Now I came to think of it, Lucy had been the only one who hadn't pestered me on the bus. It must have taken guts to come here after I brushed her off last time. She was actually OK, Lucy.

'I might do that. Thanks.'

There was another surprise awaiting me when I stepped into my form room. Right at the back of my pigeonhole was the missing ticket for the college disco night. Evidently I'd just missed it before – and it looked like the person who'd put it there had accidentally given me an extra drinks voucher too. I had to smile at that. While life wasn't great, it seems it wasn't quite as empty as I thought.

GINA BLAXILL

Rosalind
Friday 12 December, 3.00 p.m.

It started to snow during double art. I had a seat by the window and as I watched a white carpet form across the playground, I thought about the phone call I'd received yesterday. The teacher must have noticed I wasn't paying attention, but she didn't tick me off. The project I was working on – portraits inspired by retro clothing – was going well; I'd done a lot of research outside school. When people asked what had inspired it, I just shrugged.

I was no nearer to making a decision about the phone call by the time class ended. As we walked out of the main doors Abby asked, 'Do you want to come over tonight?'

'Maybe after I take the dog out.' Something caught my eye. A figure was standing over on the other side of the road, looking lost in the rush of students, and rather cold, because he wasn't wearing a coat.

'Quick.' I grabbed Abby's arm.

But he'd spotted me; he was walking over. I stood still, keeping my face as blank as I could. When he was in earshot, I said, 'Hello.'

Jonathan gave an awkward-looking smile. 'Hi. I feel stupid. It was quite warm when I left.'

'Ros,' said Abby, 'I'm off now. Text me later.'

'You can't just go—' But it was too late; she had.

Jonathan drew a breath. 'I owe you an apology. Look, do you have time to talk?'

'What's there to say? I know what you think. You said so.' And I knew he'd meant it too.

Jonathan looked unhappy. He took his hand from his pocket and fiddled with his glasses.

'Look, Ros . . . I don't fancy you. Sorry, but that's the way it is. It's got nothing to do with the way you look and it's not because I don't like you, either, cos I do. A lot.' He gave me that lopsided smile. 'I miss you. I'd like to be friends again, if you're up for it.'

Over the weeks, I'd thought about Jonathan a lot. I'd come to realize there were two ways I could go from where I was. One was to mope about feeling hurt and rejected, and the other was to get on with things. And, being sensible as usual, I'd chosen the second. I could see now that I'd expected too much from him and hoped too hard. I was always going to be disappointed. Knowing this didn't stop me wishing things had been different, of course.

'What about what I did?' I mumbled. 'I'm not proud of that.'

'Yeah, you made some bad choices and I was mad at you for a while. But I've been thinking things over and I'm not proud of how I acted either. I was a mopey pain in the arse who couldn't see what was going on under his nose, and I'm surprised you put up with me. People screw up, Ros;

we both have, but I don't see the point in griping about it two months on. Far as I'm concerned, past is past. Right?'

I thought about this, and nodded. 'Right.'

'You know something? Sounds corny, and it's embarrassing to admit . . . but since I was tiny, I wanted a little sister.'

I drew patterns on the pavement with my foot. I wished I could say something about wanting a big brother, so everything could be all right, but I couldn't quite manage it.

When I didn't answer Jonathan said, 'I've seen London. You should visit Norwich – it's a great city. I can show you round. It'll be fun.'

I gave him a long look. 'Won't you be embarrassed about being seen with a kid?'

'You can say you're my cousin or something. I'm not bothered. Course, you could just tell the truth and say you're my friend.'

I decided I might well do that. I'd told enough lies to last me a long time. 'OK. Maybe I will.'

'Friends again?'

I couldn't help smiling. 'Yeah, I guess we are.'

We started to walk along the road. It felt a little funny to be with Jonathan again, but not as weird as I'd expected.

'How have you been getting on?' I asked.

'Not bad. I'm taking music now – I dropped further maths. There was a load of work to catch up on, but I'm up to speed now. They're OK, some of the kids in my class. They'll never be my best friends but at least I have people to hang out with.'

'That's great!'

He laughed. 'Would you believe it, I wrote a song the day after we found Freya, and now I can't stop scribbling stuff down. Maybe it's a good thing she broke my heart. Half the songs you hear are about love screwing you over, so I reckon I'm on to a winner there.'

I thought about saying something about how much I'd been drawing since everything had happened, but decided not to. Even for that inspiration, I couldn't bring myself to say having my heart broken had been a good thing.

'It's funny,' Jonathan said. 'I thought Freya would leave a huge hole in my life, but it hasn't been that way. Guess I've realized I don't need her any more; I can get by just being me.' He paused. 'Actually, I've been missing you a whole lot more than Freya.'

I beamed; I couldn't help it. 'I saw Freya a little while after everything happened. Hugh called round and she was with him. They went off arm in arm – they looked happy, I guess.'

'Yeah, I heard that she's still seeing him. Kind of amusing. Her mum used to moan about me when we were going out, saying I wasn't good enough for Freya, and now suddenly I'm her favourite person, cos there's someone new to complain about. Hey, am I imagining it, or are you growing your hair?'

He noticed. 'Yeah, I thought I'd give it a go. I don't do myself favours, having it cut like a boy's.'

'I don't do myself favours by having mine cut like a girl's. Someone called me "miss" last week. Talk about mortifying.' Jonathan paused. 'I saw the police again, just after the whole Student Snatcher thing got wrapped up. They told me – off the record – all about Brian. Far as they can tell, it's pretty much what the newspapers are speculating – that classic pattern of meeting someone new, things going well, then something going wrong that led to him wanting to make them pay. Apparently Brian doesn't think he's done anything wrong – it's *their* fault for rejecting him! He must be insane. Crazy that we were mixed up in all that, isn't it? I mean – us!'

I nodded. 'It's all pretty twisted.'

We turned into my road.

'Want to come in?' I asked. 'You don't have to dash off somewhere, do you?'

'Got to meet Mum and Dad at seven; we're going to the theatre, but that's not for a while. Will your dad mind? I know he's a bit off about Internet people.'

'Jono, you stopped being an Internet person a while ago.'

'Weird that out of all the billions of people I could have ended up talking to it was you, isn't it? Scary if you think about how improbable it all is. But I guess what it does prove is that just sometimes, strangers aren't your enemies.'

He was right there. I glanced up and down the road, though there was no one listening. For a moment, I remembered the first time I shared my thoughts with Jonathan – only I hadn't known his name then, or that we'd ever speak on the phone or meet in person, or that we'd become friends. Back then my biggest concerns had been that I was losing the only mate I had and feeling that no one saw me for who I was.

I wasn't worried about either of those things any more.

'I've something I want to talk over with you actually.' It sounded abrupt, but there was no easy way to bring this up. 'Mum called yesterday. She wants to meet up.'

Jonathan whistled. 'OK, agony uncle at the ready . . .'

Acknowledgements

Pretty Twisted and myself have been on a very long journey together, but luckily for both of us we've definitely not been travelling alone. There are a number of lovely people I'd like to thank:

My agent, Becky Bagnell, for invaluable help and advice, but most of all for seeing potential in my script in the early days; the uber-helpful team at Macmillan, especially my ever-enthusiastic editor, Emma Young; my friend Matt, who talked me through CCTV; my own 'not an Internet friend any more' pal, Irina, who read the first draft and has kept interested ever since; everyone at the three workplaces I've been at since I started the book, for being so excited and optimistic on my behalf (especially team EdLi and honorary EdLi members – you know who you are!); Rudi, who didn't know I was writing a book and wouldn't have been to able to read it anyway, but provided constant, silent support; my brother, Luke, who in his usual last-minute fashion thought up the final twist; and, above all, my parents, Sheila and David, for putting up with my endless book angst for almost three years and helping me find solutions to every problem – without your love and support I've no doubt *Pretty Twisted* wouldn't have made it.

Jaclyn Moriarty

Dreaming of Amelia

The first time I saw her I knew that my Amelia was a ghost.

Amelia and Riley have transferred to Ashbury High for their final year, and the whole school is completely obsessed with them. Glamorous, gifted and totally devoted to one another, they seem to be perfect. But there's more to them than beauty and talent. Riley and Amelia have secrets. And everyone at Ashbury is about to find out that the past casts a very long shadow . . .

A NEW ERA.
A NEW BEGINNING.
A NEW LOVE.

Much of the Earth is under water. In the high mountains at the top of the world Lily's people have made a new life – but she feels trapped. Far away, beneath a soaring sky-city that towers above the ocean, the war Fox has been planning for finally begins. The world must be made whole again – but can Lily find Fox and fix the broken past?

Or will his war keep them apart?

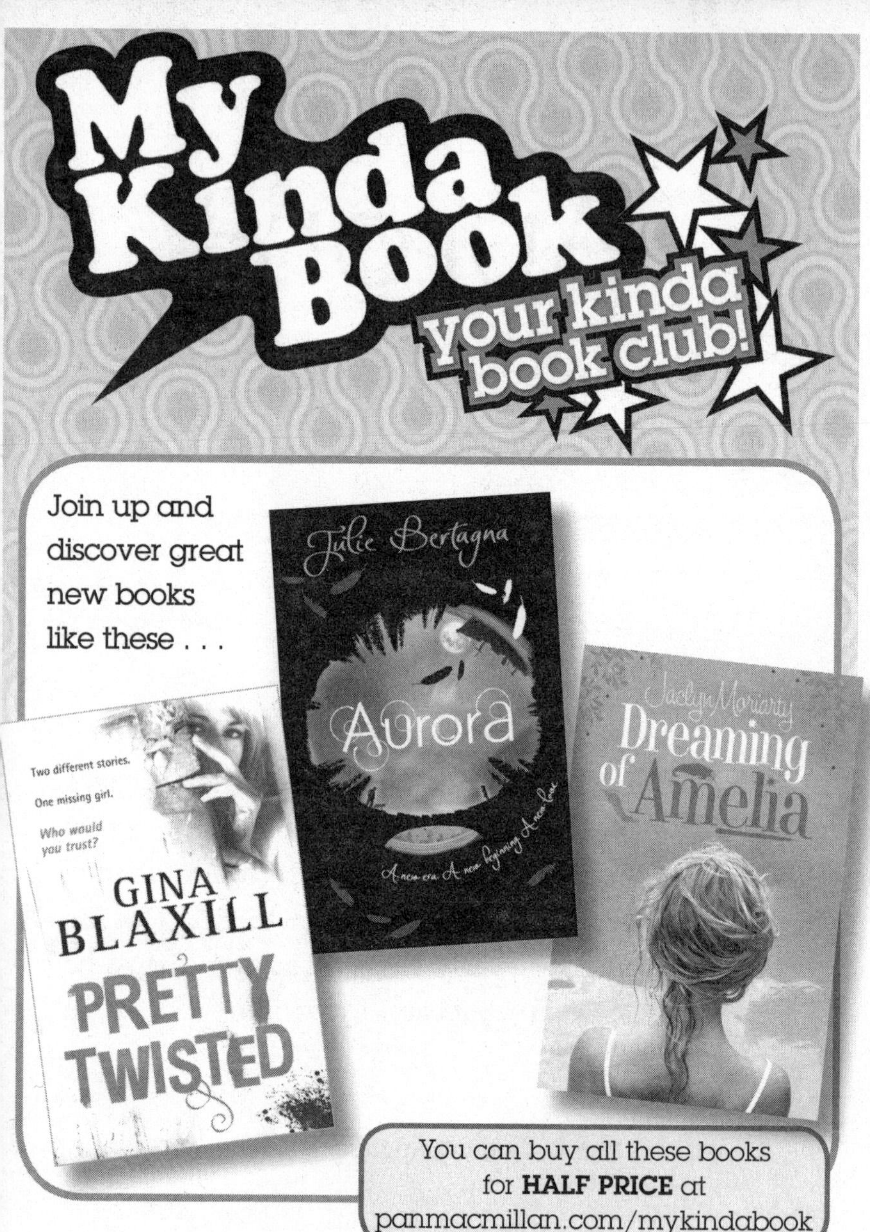

Log on to **MyKindaBook.com** to read extracts, chat to authors, win **FREE** stuff and go behind the scenes of **PRETTY TWISTED**!